The Cowboy Kid

D0896298

David A. Poulsen

A

Red　　　　　Hawk

Book

Canadian Cataloguing in Publication Data

Poulsen, David A., 1946-
    The cowboy kid

(Rodeo trilogy series;) 1
ISBN 0-9680186-1-0

I. Title.   II. Series: Poulsen David A., 1946- Rodeo trilogy series; 1
PS8581.O848C6 1995   jC813'.54   C95-911087-9
PZ7.P68Co 1995

Illustrations by John Duffy
Cover art by Treena Bryant
First published by Plains Publishing, 1987
Red Hawk first printing, 1995

Published by:
Red Hawk Communications
Box 5053
High River, Alberta T1V 1M3

Printed and bound in Canada by Friesens Books

For Murray, Amy and Brad
Who have always made me so very proud.

"In every little kid there's a cowboy
  and in every cowboy there's a little kid."

-Brian Claypool
 (1953 - 1979)

John T Duffy
'86

Chapter One

Clayton Findlay thought about trying to hide. Maybe he could conceal himself somewhere on the motionless train, at least until it pulled out of the station. As quickly as he had conceived the idea, he rejected it, realizing it would only delay the inevitable. That decision made, the boy shrugged his shoulders, glanced once more back at the railway car that had been his home for the past three and a half days, and stepped out into the Alberta sunshine.

He paused before descending the steps of the train and looked out at the faces of the crowd gathered at the station on that May afternoon. Not recognizing anyone, the slightly built passenger stepped lightly down onto the platform and began walking toward the waiting room.

"So this is it," Clayton muttered distastefully to himself, "Calgary, the heart of the golden west."

His youthful features formed a look of disdain beneath his blond, unkempt hair. Two men in stetsons, blue jeans and cowboy boots were standing nearby engaged in animated conversation.

Clayton rolled his eyes in disgust."I need this town like I need a…"

"Clayton." He turned as he heard his name called. He didn't recognize the man who was walking toward him, but then, he had been just six years old the only other time he'd seen his uncle. That had been seven years earlier.

"Good to see you boy," the rugged-featured man said as he reached out his hand.

"Uncle Roy?" Clayton had to look a long way up.

"You bet," was the reply as the two shook hands. "Let me grab that suitcase. Jenny and Josh are out putting more money in the parking meter. Hate to have us spend your first night here in a Calgary jail," Roy Douglas laughed as he took the suitcase and started toward a door marked "Exit 9th Avenue."

The boy cast a last look of disapproval at the two cowboys lounging nearby, thrust his hands into his pockets and started after his uncle.

Clayton Findlay was from Toronto. He had been born there and had spent almost all of his thirteen years in the giant, eastern Canadian city. He knew it as well as most Toronto cabbies, the result of his having spent countless hours prowling the city's widely differing areas. From the green expanse of High Park, to the noisy sidewalks of Kensington market, to the luxurious mansions of Rosedale, Clayton knew each of Toronto's different faces. He was a Torontonian and happy to be one.

Now, however, he was an unwilling traveller. With his parents off on what they referred to as "a combined business trip—second honeymoon" to such exotic locales as Singapore, Bangkok and Tokyo, Clayton had been sent west, to what he considered to be nothing less than exile.

No, he wasn't looking forward to the next few months. Adding to his unhappiness was a life-long dislike for anything rural, old-fashioned or boring. To Clayton Findlay, Calgary, Alberta, Canada was all of those, in spades.

From early childhood, he had held the notion that farm and ranch people were by-and-large an unintelligent breed whose lives consisted of nothing more than tobacco chewing, old-time fiddle

2

contests and watching the rise and fall of wheat prices.

Now he found himself forced to take up residence and even go to school among the very people who conjured up those unpleasant mental pictures.

Scrambling through the busy station a few feet behind his long-striding uncle, the boy grew more and more disgruntled. Clayton placed a well-aimed kick at a discarded Coca-Cola cup. The kick sent the plastic container zinging past his uncle's arm. Roy Douglas either didn't notice or pretended not to.

The big-boned, genial man was as different from the slender youngster trying to keep up with him as the two parts of Canada in which they lived. Roy Douglas was a product of the land he lived in. On the one hand he was as hard as the Rockies that rose suddenly out of the prairies to the west. On the other, he was capable of the gentleness of a chinook wind that often blew over those same mountains bringing a warm respite to winter's unpleasant grip.

Once he'd been a rodeo hand of better than average ability. Now he was a stock contractor, responsible for raising the feisty, four-legged critters that tested cowboys' skill and endurance in rodeo arenas all over the west. He had two hundred and forty acres of rugged ranch land situated in the foothills, ninety-five kilometers southwest of Calgary. Every dollar he had was tied up in his land and his stock contracting business. It was not an easy way of life, and fate had more than once dealt near-crippling blows to the operation. But for Roy Douglas, his wife Laura and their thirteen year-old twins, Josh and Jenny, it was the life they loved.

As Clayton and his uncle emerged from the railway station and onto the street, they were greeted again by the spring sunshine. Clayton stood blinking for a second, his eyes adjusting to the brightness. A regiment of modern skyscrapers rose before him. He was more than a little surprised at the bigness of what he had expected to be a small town. Then he saw his cousin Josh leaning against the side of a double-blue pickup truck, a battered straw cowboy hat pushed back on his head.

Josh was as much like his father as it was possible for a boy to be. He loved Alberta, the ranch, the stock and most of all — rodeo. Although the same age as Clayton, he was darker, taller and heavier than his eastern relative. Ever since he had turned ten, the age at which he had been allowed to enter his first rodeo, summer meant impatiently waiting during the week for weekends. With the weekends came the chance to compete in the Boys' Steer Riding event at whatever rodeo his dad happened to be supplying stock for.

Towns that few people knew and even fewer remembered all held recollections of battles fought on ornery steers for this young cowboy and dozens of other boys like him. Towns and cities with names like Swift Current, Okotoks, Medicine Hat, Cranbrook and countless others; each conjured up mental pictures of chute gates opening and steers suddenly exploding into twisting, leaping, gyrating action. Aboard a steer, a rider sometimes lasted the all-important eight seconds. Other times, when the animal was just too tough, the rider ended up in a cloud of dust on the ground, beaten for the moment.

Either way, those times were what Josh lived for. When the rodeo ended there was barely time for congratulations or commiserations before his attention, like that of all rodeo cowboys, turned expectantly to the next ride, in the next town, at the next rodeo.

"Josh, say hello to your cousin Clayton. It's been a long time since you guys have seen each other. Guess you probably don't remember one another," Roy said as he deposited Clayton's suitcase in the back of the truck.

Josh stood up straight, nodded and grinned shyly at his cousin. Clayton returned the nod but not the grin and turned to his uncle.

"Tell me, does everybody out here wear those hats?" he asked unpleasantly.

"Well, Clayton, the truth is," the big man replied with a laugh, "there's only two kinds of people out here—those that's cowboys and those that would like to be." He turned to Josh. "Where's Jenny?"

"I don't know Dad, she was here a minute ago."

Clayton wasn't paying particular attention at that moment as his head was thrown back to enable him to look up to the top of the Calgary Tower. Standing as he was, right alongside the circular concrete structure, it seemed as if the top was actually swaying as white wreaths of cloud drifted by far above it. Clayton was brought sharply back to earth by an interruption similar to the jarring irritation of an early morning alarm clock. This time, however, the irritant came in the form of a four-foot-six-inch, brown-eyed, red-haired package of non-stop energy. Jenny Douglas was back.

Josh's twin sister Jenny was every bit as rough and tumble and rodeo-crazy as her brother was, but that's where the similarity ended. Where Josh, like his dad, was softspoken, easy-going and usually willing to avoid an argument, Jenny could be quick-tempered, acid-tongued and liked nothing better than a good verbal scrap. Yet Jenny had a soft side. It was a side of her that people often missed, however, particularly people who failed to look beneath the girl's seemingly tough surface.

"Geez, you should have seen what I just saw," Jenny announced to the three of them. "A guy just walked by here with purple hair, at least half of it was purple and the other half was green and it was all in points. I asked him how he got it like that and..."

"You asked him?" Josh repeated.

"Sure," Jenny shrugged, "but he just told me to get a life so I told him to..."

"Jenny," her father interrupted. "You haven't said hello to Clayton yet."

"Hello," she said simply, but before Clayton could reply, his fiery cousin had returned to the subject that obviously interested her more. "You should have seen this guy, Dad, I mean, he was weird."

"I'm sure he was, Jen," was the laughing response.

"What's the big deal?" Clayton asked his cousin. "Haven't you ever seen a punker before? How far behind the times is this place anyway?"

"Well maybe we haven't got as many weirdos as you're used to," Jenny's voice rose. "He was probably from the east anyway."

"Oh, I imagine we've got our share of folks who like to look and act a little different too," Roy gently interjected as he tried to head off an early flare-up between the two.

"Thing is, we don't get into the city all that often to see 'em," Josh added and turned to open the passenger door of the truck. Jenny climbed in first and was hesitatingly followed by Clayton. Then, with Roy and Josh flanking Alberta's newest arrival and his firebrand cousin, the truck eased gently into the traffic. They made a right turn at the first intersection and headed south.

For a few minutes the foursome rode in silence. Then at a red light, Josh pointed to a stockade-type fence down the street to their left. "That's where they hold the Calgary Stampede," he explained. Clayton looked in the direction Josh was pointing but was more interested in a sleek, swift-moving rapid transit train passing in front of the stockade fence. For the second time in minutes, he was mildly surprised by the city's modern appearance. When Clayton failed to answer, Josh asked, "You've heard of the Calgary Stampede, haven't you?"

"Yes, I have," Clayton responded, "but I never paid much attention."

"Yeah, I guess somebody from the East wouldn't think much about it," Josh agreed. "But to us it's the biggest rodeo in the world so it means a lot. My goal is to compete there. If everything goes right, I'll be competing at the Calgary Stampede this year. I almost made it last year but I broke my collarbone two weeks before."

Silence again settled over the travellers and no further conversation took place as the truck left Calgary on the highway south, turned west for about a half hour and then south again on a black top road. After a few minutes, Clayton was able to relax a little and take in some of the surroundings. The terrain quickly changed from the flat, barren prairie he had been seeing from the train for the past couple of days. The road rolled over a series of gently curving hills punctuated here

and there by dense stands of slender, sturdy pop-
lar trees.

Occasionally, when the truck came up onto high
ground, the occupants were in sight of the Rockies.
Clayton could clearly see the snow that still topped
the higher peaks. It seemed to him that if his Uncle
Roy were to stop the truck, a brisk fifteen minute walk
would put them at the foot of the first mountain.

"How far away are they?" he asked, leaning forward to get a better look.

"Oh, maybe an hour's drive," Roy responded.
The boy shot a quick glance at his uncle to see if he
was pulling his leg.

Inwardly, Clayton was spellbound by the beauty
of the postcard-like scenes. Outwardly, he was determined to display no interest in anything the Canadian West had to offer. He leaned back in his seat
and did his best to look bored.

Eventually the truck slowed and turned off onto
a gravel driveway. Clayton looked at the sign beside the turnoff. It had a capital D and then another
on its side.

Noticing the boy's intent study of the sign, his
uncle said, "That's our brand. We call this place the
D Lazy D. Putting a letter on its side like that in a
brand means you call it `lazy.' My dad named the
place when he first bought it twenty-five years ago.
The first D is for his name Douglas and the lazy D,
well that's for me `cause I guess that's about what I
amounted to in those days." He laughed as he
steered the truck into the driveway and stopped in
front of a two-storey blue and white house set
amidst a ring of pine trees.

As the truck stopped, Josh jumped out to be
greeted by a barking, jumping, furry bundle known

8

to the Douglas family as Casey. Casey was what was referred to as a "Heinz 57" dog, meaning he was as far from a purebred as a dog could get. But he was completely faithful to each member of the Douglas family. In fact, he was considered by most of the neighbours and the Douglases themselves to be a full-fledged member of the family.

As Clayton stepped from the truck, the dog stopped playing with Josh and eyed this stranger carefully. As capable a watchdog as any farm dog around, Casey was instinctively on guard against a possible intruder. Clayton slowly bent down, held out a hand toward the dog and said quietly, "What's his name?"

"We call him Casey," Josh replied as he, Jenny and their dad watched Clayton and the dog with interest.

Clayton didn't move toward the dog but continued to hold out his hand. Then softly he said, "Come here Casey, come here boy, come on big fella, I just want to meet you." Casey took a hesitant step toward the outstretched hand and then stopped, his eyes never leaving the face of the newcomer. "It's all right, Casey, nothing to worry about, come here now," the boy coaxed. The dog stepped closer and sniffed Clayton's hand. Still the boy didn't move. "That's right. Good fella. That's right Casey, you check me out and see if I'm okay. Take your time boy, that's right."

Finally, the long, shaggy tail began to move, slowly at first, then more quickly and finally with the enthusiastic wag of a dog that felt he was with someone to be trusted. The boy ruffled the fur on the big dog's neck and stood up.

His Uncle Roy spoke, "It looks like you made a

good impression. He doesn't usually have much use for strangers at first."

"I get along fine with dogs," Clayton said simply and turned and walked toward the house.

Josh and Jenny looked at one another and frowned, obviously not able to understand their cousin or what it was that seemed to be bothering him.

Roy reached into the back of the truck and removed his nephew's suitcase. The three Douglases and Casey followed their guest up to the house.

The door opened and Laura Douglas stepped out onto the porch. She was a small woman with auburn hair and a pretty face that radiated kindness. "Well," she said with a warm smile, "this must be Clayton. I hardly recognize you, it's been so long." She held the door open and gestured for Clayton to go into the house. She followed him inside with Roy and Josh right behind them. Jenny had taken a detour to the barn. "I just took a roast out of the oven so how would you like some nice, hot, roast beef sandwiches? I bet you're starved."

"Not really," Clayton replied, "but I guess I wouldn't mind a sandwich."

"How about us," Roy chimed in, "or is that roast just for visitors?"

"Well, normally it would just be for visitors," Laura teased, "but I guess I can make an exception for a couple of scrawny characters like you."

Roy and the two boys sat down at the table. Casey stood alongside Clayton as the boy ran his fingers through the dog's thick, brown fur.

The sandwiches were ready in a minute and Roy and Josh attacked them with considerable enthusiasm. Clayton, after a halfhearted attempt at a couple of bites said, "I wonder if you could excuse me. I guess I'm not really hungry. Could you tell me where my room is?"

"Certainly, Clayton," Aunt Laura answered, "Josh, why don't you show Clayton where to put his things."

"Sure," Josh mumbled in reply, his mouth still engaged in consuming the last of a sandwich.

"That's okay. I can find it if you just point the way."

Josh slowly sat back down as his mother said, "Of course Clayton. Up the stairs and it's the second door on your left."

Without a reply, the boy left the room. For a few minutes Josh and Roy continued to eat in silence. Finally Josh spoke, "He doesn't seem very glad to be here, does he Dad?"

Roy looked at his son for a minute and said, "Well, Josh, think about it this way. Suppose all of a sudden you had to live in a place that was completely different from anything you're familiar with here at home. How do you think you would feel about it?"

"Yeah, I see what you mean," Josh nodded. "It would take some getting used to, all right."

"I think he'll be okay if we give him a little time," Roy added. "Did you see how he hit it off with Casey? Anybody that has a way with animals like that boy seems to have is going to fit in just fine out here. But we'll have to be patient and let him get used to us in his own way, and in his own time. Now one more sandwich and then you better go help your sister with the chores."

Josh nodded in ready agreement and reached for the platter.

Chapter Two

Clayton opened his eyes, and for a second wondered where he was. Then, as his mind became fully alert, he remembered his arrival at the Douglas ranch. He lay in bed and looked around at the room that was to be his for the next few months. It was clean and bright with floral wallpaper on two of the walls. The third wall, at the head of his bed, featured a large tapestry of two horses in full gallop over a lush green field, with a clear emerald-blue stream in the background. Clayton studied the tapestry and marveled at the well-muscled forms of the two horses. He thought to himself how well the artist had captured the magnificence and freedom of the animals.

His attention was directed to the open window on the far side of the room and the sound of voices outside. Getting out of bed, he went to the window and looked down to see his uncle Roy and Josh saddling a big chestnut horse. For a moment, Clayton's still sleepy mind wondered if he was expected to ride to school on horseback. Then he remembered the only good news he had received during the day before. His arrival coincided with the district's annual teacher's convention. That meant he would be spared, for the moment at least, the unpleasantness of his first day in what he was sure would be a one-room school, complete with a pot-bellied stove and an outhouse.

Below, Casey had joined the group in the yard. Clayton smiled to himself as he watched the dog dart forward, then back and repeat the process as if to get his masters to hurry their preparations and get started on their way.

Turning back from the window, Clayton dressed quickly. He didn't like the idea of having to be on the ranch but as long as he was there, he disliked even more the idea of being left behind when something was going on.

He ambled down the stairs and through the kitchen, only shaking his head as Aunt Laura greeted him cheerfully and offered toast and cereal. Jenny was sitting at the kitchen table but her attention was directed at a bowl of cereal and she didn't look up. Clayton walked out the back door just as Josh was climbing into the saddle aboard the chestnut.

Hearing the slam of the screen door, Roy turned and saw his nephew lounging on the porch. Casey noticed him too and bounded up the stairs with a welcoming series of barks and tail-wagging.

"Morning, Clayton," Roy grinned, "Get a good rest?" Clayton shrugged and bent down to scratch behind Casey's floppy ears.

"I'm just going over to cut out half a dozen bulls we're sending to a rodeo school in Lethbridge," his uncle told him. "Josh is heading out to check fences. You can go with him or you can give me a hand, or if you'd rather, you can just take it easy around the house today."

"Doesn't matter to me," Clayton replied, his voice expressionless.

"Well, in that case, maybe you can help me out with those bulls," Roy said. "Jenny's going to the neighbor's to work her barrel racing horse and I could use a little help." Turning to Josh, he said, "Make sure you have a good look at that section along the north edge, and stop in and see how Hector is doing. You should be back here by noon."

"Right. See ya later Clayton," Josh waved and was off, urging the rangy chestnut horse into a casual lope. Casey, happy to be underway at last, ran easily along behind him.

"Right this way," Roy pointed, and started out on foot with Clayton almost forced to trot in order to keep up.

Clayton was curious about who Hector was, but decided against asking his uncle. They walked past several corrals, some occupied by horses and some by cattle. A big, impatient looking jet black horse with a white star between his piercing eyes stood in the last corral. The horse loped to the edge of the corral and snorted as he peered intently at them over the top rail.

"Settle down, Doc," Roy spoke easily to the snorting, pawing animal. "You've already been fed and I don't have time right now to socialize. That's Doc Holliday," he told Clayton, who had stopped walking and was returning the long stare of the magnificent horse.

"He's our stud horse, our stallion," Roy explained. "With his size and strength, we think by breeding him to fast, athletic-type mares, we should get some outstanding bucking horses. His first crop of colts will be bucking this year so we're pretty eager to see if we had the right idea. He was a great bucking horse in his day. Put a lot of cowboys on the ground, me included. Didn't ya Hotshot?" Roy laughed heartily and was off again.

It wasn't until he had gone a short distance further and turned to speak to Clayton that he noticed the boy was no longer alongside him. Looking back, he spotted Clayton still at the corral that held Doc Holliday. The boy was standing on the bottom rail

14

of the fence so that his head was above the top rail and his face just inches from that of the black stallion.

Roy Douglas walked slowly back to where Clayton and the horse were intently eyeing one another.

"Best be careful, son, he's a stud. They can be unpredictable and he could hurt you," Roy cautioned.

"No," the boy replied quietly, but without a trace of doubt. "He won't hurt me." For a long time the three of them stood motionless. Roy studied the horse and this seemingly doleful youngster from the East. The boy did not utter a sound, nor did the horse, yet Roy was horseman enough to know that there was greater communication between Clayton and Doc Holliday than if either had been expressing himself aloud.

Finally Roy spoke. "We better get up to those bulls now, Clayton." The boy slowly turned away from the horse and silently followed his uncle up a path leading away from Doc Holliday's corral. Soon they rounded a large, aging barn and came to another corral. This time Clayton stopped dead in his tracks and took a deep breath.

"That's them?" he whispered.

"That's them," his uncle replied. "They're really something aren't they?"

"People ride those?" the boy inquired incredulously.

"They try," was the answer.

Clayton took a few tentative steps closer but was careful to keep a respectful distance between himself and the enclosure. As he drew nearer, his amazement grew. In the corral were about thirty of the biggest, meanest-looking animals he had ever seen. Most of them were standing or walking slowly around. They all had their attention firmly fixed on the two visitors to the corral. Clayton had the uneasy feeling that any one of the beasts would have enjoyed nothing better than running over him at full speed, using its horns to rearrange forever his entire bone structure. Reading the boy's mind, Roy placed a big hand on his nephew's shoulder.

"Bucking bulls take some getting used to," he said. "Some are docile, some are vicious. I guess they're a lot like people in that respect. The thing to remember is to never do anything foolish or careless around one, because most times, they won't let you get away with your mistake. If you treat them with the proper amount of respect, and by that I mean respect for what they can do to you if you're careless, you won't have any problems. Come on, I'll show you what we have to do." Roy led the way to a smaller, empty corral adjoining the big one containing the bulls.

"I want you to stand right here by this gate," he explained. "I'm going to go into that pen with the bulls and cut out the ones we're shipping to the rodeo school. When I yell, you open the gate and let the bull into this pen. You'll always be behind the gate so you'll be safe but if a bull looks like he might want to get after you, climb up on the fence. You got it?"

Clayton swallowed and nodded slowly. "I think so," he said in a voice that displayed little confidence. Clayton positioned himself at the gate to the smaller pen and his uncle, armed only with a whip, made his way into the corral holding several tons of cantankerous beef. Clayton watched intently as his uncle, never straying far from the fence, made his way carefully around the herd. In a minute he had closed in on one of the bulls destined for Lethbridge. Using the whip and plenty of shouting, Roy began the process of coaxing that bull out of the herd and toward the gate manned by Clayton.

"Jubilee, get over there, yaa," the big man yelled, cracking the whip above the bull's back.

Clayton spotted the bull called Jubilee, a massive, white bull with horns that pointed downwards. Uncle Roy continued to maneuver the bull toward Clayton's gate, always taking care not to leave too much open ground between himself and the fence.

"Yaa, Bull, yaa," he called and cracked the whip again near the reluctant Jubilee's enormous flank. Gradually Jubilee and one other animal, a smaller brown bull with a white face, separated from the herd and began moving in Clayton's direction.

"Okay, Clayton, open the gate." Uncle Roy instructed, "I'm going to try to get the white bull through first. Be ready to close the gate fast before the other bull can follow him but if he keeps coming, let him in. Don't try to stop him with the gate."

Clayton opened the gate and stood in behind it. Jubilee did exactly as he was supposed to and trotted through. The brown bull moved forward as if to follow him, but Roy lunged toward him, waving his arms and hollering.

Clayton quickly shut the gate, pushed the bar across and yelled, "Yaa, Bull, yaa," following his uncle's example. The brown bull stopped, looked at the closed gate, turned quietly around and ambled off.

Roy jumped up on the gate. "Just right, Clayton," he grinned, "Anybody'd think you've been doing this all your life."

A grin began to form on Clayton's face, but he caught himself. "Being a cowboy isn't that tough," he said unpleasantly.

His uncle shook his head and climbed down from the gate. He decided to say nothing about the boy's reluctance to enjoy his new life in the west. If Clayton was happy, he seemed determined not to let anyone see it.

"We've got five more to go, Clayton. We'll just do it the same way, but remember there's a bull behind you now. Jubilee's all right; he probably won't bother you but just be aware of him. We don't send our rank bulls to rodeo schools so most of these aren't too bad. There's one that's a bit of a bad actor, so we'll leave him to the last."

Roy explained that the five bulls still to be cut out were Rio Bravo, Sledgehammer, King Tut, Ace High and Little Bighorn, the troublesome bull that would be left to the end.

Three quarters of an hour later, the first four had been sorted into the smaller corral almost as easily as Jubilee had been. The only incident was a threatening snort from Ace High as he went through the gate. The snort, accompanied by a menacing glare at Clayton, had sent a shiver down the boy's spine. Then the bull continued on to join the others which were soon to be bound for Lethbridge.

Now it was time for Little Bighorn. But if Roy and his nephew had expected problems, the bull was to give them a surprise. It was as if the nasty-looking, blue-grey bull with the large brahma hump on his back had read a manual of etiquette. The stock contractor had no sooner approached the group of four bulls in which Little Bighorn was standing, than the bull emerged from the group and

18

sidled nonchalantly toward Clayton. The boy opened the gate and Little Bighorn ambled in.

Clayton closed the gate and climbed up on the fence to survey the morning's work. The six bulls were standing quietly in the pen, ready to be loaded on a truck and taken to Lethbridge. There, aspiring young bullriders would climb on, get bucked off and climb on again.

Roy stepped up alongside his nephew. "Well, that's it for now," he told the boy. "I don't know about you but I could use a cup of coffee and maybe a piece of hot apple pie. How about it?"

"Sure," Clayton replied. He jumped down and started to cut across the corral. It happened quickly and without warning. Little Bighorn, the bull that had been standing quietly just seconds earlier, turned, and with head down, charged. Roy yelled and Clayton turned to see the rampaging animal bearing down on him. He turned quickly and dashed for the fence but the distance was too great and the bull too fast. The outcome was inevitable.

At the last possible instant, Roy, who had leaped from the fence when the bull began its charge, dashed between the animal and its fleeing victim. It was a momentary distraction, the kind that rodeo clowns provide as they enable bull riders to escape to safety. It was momentary, but it was enough.

Clayton made the fence, jumped up and looked back. His feeling of relief quickly turned to horror. He saw that the bull had turned its attention now to his uncle. As Roy attempted to dodge Little Bighorn's charge, he slipped and went down. Instantly, he was back up on his feet and resumed his run for safety. But the fall had given the bull just the amount of time it needed. Little Bighorn lowered his head and slammed his right horn against Roy's leg. Clayton watched helplessly as his uncle went down a second time. Hurt and unable to get back up, Roy tried to roll for the fence. The bull hesitated, then lowered his head and prepared for another charge at the defenseless cowboy.

At that moment everything began happening at once. Just as Little Bighorn took aim at his prey, a snarling, snapping miniature hurricane erupted beneath the bull. It was Casey, and the dog was darting, barking, leaping back, growling and leaping forward again. The enormous creature that towered over him was confused and annoyed.

Josh appeared right behind Casey. He hollered and waved his arms and added to Little Bighorn's general confusion. Finally, with a haughty toss of his massive head as if to signal he had had enough of this crazy pair, the bull turned and trotted away with Casey providing a few last nips and snarls for good measure.

Josh ran to his Dad's assistance and helped him to the fence and safety. Once outside the corral, Roy lay on his back, gulping for air, as his concerned son looked on.

"You all right, Dad?" he asked.

"I think so, Josh, just a charleyhorse, I think. He gave me one good shot in there before you and Casey arrived on the scene. That was good work, Son. Thanks. That goes for you, too," the big man said as he reached over and gave Casey a grateful rub.

"I busted a stirrup leather and had to come back early. I guess it was a good thing," Josh grinned.

"First time I've ever been glad for broken tack," Roy nodded ruefully as he struggled to his feet. He had to lean on Josh's shoulder to stand up.

Clayton, who had been frozen in terror as the drama had been enacted before him, slowly approached his uncle. "I...I'm sorry," he stammered.

Roy looked at his nephew. "Forget it, Clayton. It's nothing. Just a bruise most likely. I guess we both learned never to take a bull for granted, didn't we?"

"But you'd just finished telling me to be careful. You must think I'm a real jerk. I should have never come here. I don't belong here. I'll never belong here." Clayton's voice rose until he was shouting. "I don't want to be here anyway!" As he finished he ran off in the direction of the house. He didn't wait for an answer.

Roy started to call after him and then changed his mind.

"Still think he's going to fit in fine?" Josh inquired dubiously of his father.

Roy looked down at his son. "Clayton made a big mistake just now and he's embarrassed about it. Heck, I've pulled a few dandies myself over the years and so have you, so let's not be too hard on him." The injured cowboy gingerly tested his leg. "Now get me up to the house so we can get that stirrup leather fixed and get you back out on fence patrol. You're not getting out of work this easily."

Clayton had reached the house and burst through the back door. He ran past Aunt Laura as she was pulling a pie out of the oven. "Clayton, what's wrong?" she asked.

Clayton didn't slow down. He bolted up the stairs, and slammed his bedroom door behind him for an answer. Laura put the steaming pie down on the counter and rushed to the back steps. She could see her husband leaning on Josh as they slowly worked their way toward the house. Roy had one arm around his son's shoulders for support but managed to wave to his wife that he was okay.

Upstairs, Clayton flung open the closet door and grabbed his suitcase. He couldn't go home to Toronto, but he wasn't going to stay at the D Lazy D either. As he whirled around to put the suitcase on the bed, he knocked a lamp off a bedside table. The base of the lamp, shaped like a saddle, broke off and smashed into what looked like a thousand tiny pieces.

"Oh no," Clayton threw himself on the bed. "I can't do anything right. I'm no good to anybody, not even myself!"

JOHN T Duffy

Chapter 3

It was only a couple of days before Roy was able to get around almost normally, sporting only a slight limp.

Clayton had spent most of the weekend in self-imposed solitary confinement, joining the others only at mealtimes. He didn't want to walk down the stairs and through the house with his suitcase and there always seemed to be at least one member of the family around to question his escape. So he resigned himself to life at the ranch, at least for the moment. He spoke only to answer questions and responded halfheartedly to the playful enticements of Casey. The dog had taken a definite shine to the ranch's newest resident.

Clayton's worst moment was provided by the irrepressible Jenny who couldn't resist the opportunity to give her eastern kin what she considered to be a well-deserved verbal slap.

"It's bad enough that somebody's been doin' their darndest to put us out of business," she had vented her anger over dinner. "Now we've got our own family helpin' 'em by nearly gettin' Dad killed."

Clayton, for his part, was tempted to ask what she meant by the remark about somebody trying to put the D Lazy D out of business, but chose instead to leave the table and return to his room. He wasn't prepared yet to start showing interest in the place. Clayton was especially determined to ignore any words that came from the mouth of one particular member of the Douglas family.

When he finally left the prison of his bedroom, it was straight for the corrals. He wanted to see the black horse. From his perch atop the fence that formed the horse's corral, the boy shared his private thoughts with the one being he trusted.

"They don't understand me. I know they don't, none of 'em. My folks don't understand me or they'd never have sent me somewhere I don't want to be. And these people, they don't understand me either. How could they? They don't know anything about the way I'm used to living. I mean, they're nice enough people, except for Jenny, of course," Clayton admitted. "Aunt Laura treats me great and Uncle Roy and Josh are okay but they don't want me here. They're cowboys and I'm not. And I don't wanna be one."

The conversation was always much the same. Clayton spoke in a hushed, confidential voice and the horse stood patiently and listened while the boy's hand repeatedly ran through the black, unruly mane.

"I know I don't fit in. She was right. I could've gotten Uncle Roy killed by that stupid bull. Why did I have to come here? You understand, don't ya, Doc? Well, at least I've got one friend, right fella?"

In this way, an unlikely union was formed — between a horse that previously had cared for no man and a boy who, though a stranger to the world of horses, sought and found friendship in the spirited stallion.

When it was time for the students of the area to return to school, Clayton was pleasantly surprised by the size and modern appearance of the almost new school building. He wound up in the same room as Josh and Jenny. Never an overly enthusiastic student, the part he enjoyed most was the half hour bus ride to and from the school which was located in the town of High River. The long bouncing journey each way was a striking contrast to his former route to and from school, a four block walk on Bloor Street, one of Toronto's busiest and most exciting streets.

Clayton's first couple of days at the school were made memorable by the antics of Jenny. Determined to make her cousin's first days at his new school unforgettable, she used tried and true methods — placing a thumb tack on his desk seat and while Clayton's attention was diverted by Josh, tying his shoelace to the corner of the desk. Her moment of glory came, however, on the second day, when Clayton plunged his hand into his lunch bag. The squeal that followed as the boy made his first "hands-on" acquaintance with a particularly large garter snake had Jenny and her circle of friends giggling through the entire noon hour.

While Clayton was a stranger to the west, he was no tenderfoot when it came to getting revenge. That afternoon, Jenny, who took great pride in her school work, was asked to read out her answer to a math problem that had been assigned for homework the previous day. She turned to the appropriate page in her workbook with her usual self-assurance. Suddenly her confidence turned to confusion and then to panic as she scrambled through the workbook looking for the page. But it was gone! In fact, all of the pages with last night's homework were missing!

"They they were… right here," the helpless girl sputtered, her face rapidly assuming the same color as her hair. Her embarrassment increased even more as she received an unaccustomed reprimand from the teacher.

Then, from his seat two ahead of her and one row over, Clayton turned to her and smiled angelically.

"Tsk, tsk, you really ought to do your homework, you know," he whispered loudly enough that most of the students were able to hear. Realizing what had happened, Jenny's face contorted with fury.

Her mood wasn't helped any by the barely concealed laughter of her classmates as Clayton turned back to the front, raised his hand and said politely, "I can give you the answer to that, Mrs. Phipps, I have it right here." There on his desk, neatly clipped down one side were the missing pages from Jenny's notebook.

When her anger finally cooled, Jenny herself had to admit the prank had been a good one and thereafter an unspoken truce existed between the two cousins — at least at school.

Clayton came to recognize the landmarks of the twice daily school bus ride. The gaudily painted granaries of the McLeod farm were first and always brought a smile, so different were they from the dull gray-silver of everyone else's granaries. A little further east lay what was left of Holy Dinah church. All that remained was a rock foundation and a few grown-over graves. The place's unlikely name was derived from the original — Holy Dynasty. The children of the district had, a half century before, shortened it to the more manageable Holy Dinah. Fire had destroyed the building some fifteen years ago, but the name still stuck.

Then came the inviting Fishermen's Heaven, a gently undulating stream that ran north and south and was, Josh assured his cousin, true to its name. And finally there was Lucky's Meadow, which was the one place for which no one seemed to be able to relate the origin of the name. It was the site of a rancher's baseball tournament every August. And always, to the west, the mountains, providing that incredible backdrop for all that lay before them. Yes, it was a far cry from Bloor Street.

A few days later, Clayton awoke to the sound of frenzied activity in the house below and outside in the yard. Getting out of bed, he crossed to the window and looked down on the scene below. Two unfamiliar pick-up trucks were parked in the yard, one with a horse trailer attached and the other with a large camper perched on it. Uncle Roy was talking with three cowboys while another man was maneuvering a huge stock liner back against a ramp leading from one of the corrals.

In a few minutes Clayton was dressed and downstairs. Walking casually into the kitchen, he attempted to sound as uninterested as possible as he asked, "What's going on?"

Aunt Laura, who was loading what seemed like an endless supply of sandwiches into a cooler, turned and smiled, "We're off to Taber for the rodeo there." She replied. "It's a three-day show and the first performance is tonight. We'll be on the road as soon as the stock is loaded. Mrs. Phipps knows that you will be missing from school." Turning back to her task, she added, "I guess this will be your first rodeo, won't it? It should be quite an experience for you."

Not at all convinced, Clayton stepped out onto the back porch to get a closer look at the goings-on. Two of the strangers and Josh were in the corral directing bucking horses up the ramp and into the liner. Uncle Roy was still talking with one of the other cowboys. When his uncle noticed Clayton on the porch, he waved an arm in the boy's direction.

"Come on over here, Clayton, I'd like you to meet somebody. This is Ben Bradley. He lives up the highway a little way. Ben is probably about the best pickup man there is. Ben and the boys come over and give us a hand loading stock when we're getting ready for a rodeo." Ben Bradley smiled and nodded at Clayton, who did not acknowledge the greeting. "This'll be Clayton's first trip down the road," Roy told Ben.

"Should be a good one," Ben observed. "Did you hear who drew Bad Medicine?"

"Nope," Roy shook his head.

"Lefty Shivers," Ben told him and both men grinned.

Noting Clayton's uncomprehending look, his uncle explained, "Bad Medicine is what you might call a once-in-a-lifetime bull. We've been bucking him for three years and he's never been ridden. Not even at the Canadian Finals. Lefty Shivers, well now he's just about the cockiest..."

"Yappiest," interjected Ben.

"...conceited, son-of-a-buck ever to pull on chaps," Roy finished the description. "He told me once that the only reason Bad Medicine has never been ridden is because he's never drawn him. I guess we'll find out now. I'll tell you one thing though, if he does ride the bull, he'll win the rodeo easily. Come on Ben, let's get the stock loaded, I'm looking forward to Taber, Alberta." Roy and Ben headed off toward the stock liner.

Clayton's eyes followed them and he muttered, "Who cares if Lefty whatever-his-name-is rides Bad Medicine or not? Not me, that's for sure."

He turned and wandered back into the house. Aunt Laura was putting the finishing touches to a massive pot of chili. "Would you like breakfast, Clayton? There's cereal in that cupboard there, and lots of bread for toast," she invited.

"No thanks," the boy shook his head. "What's a pick-up man?"

"Pick-up men are mounted cowboys who are in the arena during the Bareback and Bronc Riding events. Their job is to move in alongside the rider after his eight seconds are up and get him off the bucking horse and safely on the ground. Then they get the bucking horse out of the arena before the next ride. It's an important job and a dangerous one too, sometimes."

At that moment, the door opened and Josh and Casey crashed into the kitchen. Seeing his mother's frown, Josh quickly said, "Sorry, Mom, I guess I was in too much of a hurry." Then, noticing the bubbling mixture on the stove, he added, "You wouldn't happen to need somebody to test that chili, would you?"

Laura smiled and said, "That's exactly what I need. You know anybody that would be interested in the job?"

"Sure do," Josh grinned. He grabbed a bowl and watched approvingly as his mother ladled some of the hot food into it.

"How about you, Clayton?" Aunt Laura asked. "Are you up to chili this early in the day?"

"No, thanks," the boy mumbled, shaking his head.

"By the way, Clayton," Josh began, "Dad and I were wondering if you might like to ride down to Taber with Ben and me in the first liner. We'll be getting there ahead of Dad and the others and we could use some help getting the horses unloaded."

Clayton stared at the floor and didn't answer.

Josh saw his reaction. "Look, I know you feel bad about what happened with Little Bighorn, but forget about it. It could have happened to anybody. We really do need help when we get there and I'd really appreciate it if you would come along with Ben and me."

"I don't need your sympa..." Clayton began but stopped in mid-sentence. He couldn't understand this cousin who actually enjoyed spending his life among cattle, horses, and small towns. Still, he didn't seem like a bad guy, everything considered. Besides, riding in the cab of the big truck might not be so bad. Finally, he said slowly, "All right, I guess I could give you a hand."

"Great," Josh shouted and instantly fell to eating his chili with a vengeance.

"Maybe I could test a little of that chili after all, Aunt Laura," Clayton said, his eyes on his cousin's steaming bowl.

"Good idea," his aunt replied. "Looks like you'll be needing it now."

Clayton pulled out a chair, sat down and asked, "Uh...where's Jenny going to ride?"

"She's already left," Josh answered between mouthfuls. "She headed out early with Cindy McKannin and her parents. They're most likely there already."

"Jenny and Cindy both barrel race and they wanted to get there early to start getting their horses used to the arena," Mrs Douglas filled in.

Clayton breathed a sigh of relief. He did not look forward to a lengthy ride in the same truck with his barb-tongued cousin. And, heck, a rodeo just might be fun.

Chapter Four

For the first couple of hours, the liner moved steadily south along Highway 2. Clayton kept his eyes riveted to the west where the distant peaks rose to meet the frothy white clouds and fell away to become a series of smaller giants. The boy thought they looked like grown horses and colts, the smaller of them wishing they were full-grown but having to wait for their time to come. It's like that for people too, he thought, but at least with mountains and horses they aren't forced to be something they don't want to be.

When they got to a town called Fort Macleod, the travellers turned east, and after passing through the coulees of Lethbridge, they came to flatter, more barren-looking land. At a sign that indicated they were nearing Taber, Ben Bradley pointed to the fields on both sides. "In a couple of months, most of this land will be covered with corn, some of the best you've ever eaten. Soon they passed what looked like two huge factories surrounded by what appeared to be mounds of dirt lumps.

"Sugar beets," explained Ben, who seemed to enjoy the role of tour guide. "This is the sugar capital of the world. The buildings are where they refine sugar, just like you what put on your cereal."

It was only a few minutes later that the liner pulled into Taber. Clayton couldn't contain the feeling of anticipation that flowed through him. Clayton, Ben and Josh went directly to the arena where dirt now covered the floor surface that had been ice all winter. Once there, they quickly unloaded the horses, leaving Clayton some time before the rodeo to soak up the atmosphere of the arena. He was aware of a mixture of smells. There was the dominant smell which reminded him of the barn at the D Lazy D. Strangely, for a young man who had spent virtually all of his life in the city, Clayton did not mind the animal smell in the barn, nor did he mind it here in the rodeo arena.

There were other smells, too—the hint of leather, the sawdust, the dirt and in the background a charcoal aroma coming from the concession stands as countless hamburgers and hot dogs were being prepared. All of it combined to provide a unique but not unpleasant smell that seemed to be everywhere in the building.

From the corrals located just outside the far end of the arena came the sounds of the stock: the bawls and bellows of the cattle and the occasional whinny of the more patient horses.

Looking around the stands, Clayton was surprised at the array of costumes. Cowboy hats and boots were in abundance as was to be expected, but they were by no means the only form of costume. Leather jackets, suits and even fur coats were sprinkled here and there through the seats of the gaudily painted arena.

So far there had been no sign of Jenny, and Clayton wasn't about to go out of his way to look for her. Just prior to the start of the rodeo, Clayton noticed Ben engaged in an animated conversation with Uncle Roy. Then, both men turned and ran off in the direction of the corrals. It was into those corrals that Clayton had helped Josh and Ben Bradley unload the horses. He knew that his Uncle Roy would have put the bulls there too. For a minute, Clayton's curiosity piqued him again, but with all the excitement of the pre-rodeo activity, he soon forgot all about the actions of the two older men.

Clayton's first rodeo was a memorable one. He stood wide-eyed through much of it. The rodeo started, as most rodeos do, with a pageant called the Grand Entry. Many of the cowboys and cowgirls, all mounted on horseback and some carrying flags, rode around the arena in an intricate pattern known as the serpentine. Then, all the riders came to a halt for the National Anthem and the reading of the Cowboy Prayer by one of the Boys' Steer Riders. All in all, Clayton had to admit to himself that it had been colourful and even a little moving.

The rodeo itself started with the most bizarre scene Clayton had ever witnessed. Three-man teams tried to saddle, mount and ride untamed, never-before-ridden mustangs the length of the arena. It was exciting, dangerous and sometimes hilarious. The announcer referred to these few minutes of frenzied, action-packed chaos as the Wild Horse Race. In spite of himself, Clayton couldn't keep from laughing out loud at the antics and spills of the contestants.

The Bareback Riding event followed and Clayton watched in genuine fascination as the Douglas Rodeo horses unleashed their power from the moment the chute gate opened. He marvelled too, at the athletic and courageous work of the cowboys who rode them, or in some cases, *tried* to ride them. The boy was especially pleased when a horse called Holliday Inn tossed its rider to the ground in short order. Clayton guessed from the name that it had to be one of Doc Holliday's offspring.

Clayton could see Ben Bradley working in the arena. Ben sat quietly on a good-looking sorrel horse and was virtually unnoticed. Then at the end of each ride when the horn sounded, he swooped in to pluck the cowboy from his bucking horse and drop him safely to the ground.

Uncle Roy was very a much part of the action too, sometimes in the arena, sometimes behind the chutes, always directing traffic and keeping the activity running smoothly. He spoke quietly but there was never any doubt who was in charge.

Steer Wrestling, known to the cowboys as Bulldogging, followed the Bareback Riding. In this event, big, strong cowboys leaped from their fast-moving horses on to the backs of steers that outweighed the contestants by three or four times. The cowboy brought the hard-charging steer to a halt, and then twisted it to the ground.

Next came the Saddle Bronc Riding. Clayton watched enthralled as riders rhythmically rode and spurred the high leaping horses with a smooth, fluid motion, in sharp contrast to the wild, jerking style of the Bareback Riding event. He had to agree with the rodeo announcer who had referred to the Saddle Bronc Riding as "the Classic" of rodeo events.

Then it was the girls' turn in the arena for the Barrel Racing event. Three barrels were set up in the arena, two at one end and one at the other. The girls had to turn a figure eight around the first two barrels, then ride to the far end of the arena, make a turn around the far barrel, then ride full-out back between the first two barrels and across a finish line to complete a cloverleaf pattern.

Clayton's interest was immediately heightened when the first girl was introduced as thirteen year-old Cindy McKannin. Clayton had seen her at school and knew she was Jenny's friend. As she made her appearance in the arena, he was surprised to note how pretty and feminine-looking she was, as unlike his rough-and-ready cousin as it was possible to be.

He found himself silently pulling for the young contestant and was pleased when she had completed the cloverleaf pattern in what the announcer called "a lightning-fast 14.53 seconds."

Clayton wasn't sure how to react when, moments later, Jenny, during her run, knocked over one of the three barrels which resulted in a five second penalty. Actually, Clayton felt a momentary pang of regret over his cousin's misfortune and even a slight twinge of guilt at having hoped, for a second at least, for that very result. The knocked down barrel would, however, provide handy ammunition if she should carry on any more about the incident with the bull Little Bighorn and for that Clayton was quite happy.

Then it was intermission time and Clayton wandered in behind the chutes where the youngest cowboys were making their final preparations. The Boys' Steer Riding was to be the second event after intermission, right after Calf Roping. Clayton found Josh putting resin on his bull-rope, which he had tied to a fence.

"You scared?" Clayton asked.

"Not really scared," Josh replied, "A little nervous maybe. I need to do well at just about every rodeo between now and the Calgary Stampede to make sure I'll qualify to ride there."

"What do you mean, 'do well'?" Clayton asked. "Don't you just try not to fall off?"

"No, there's more to it than that," Josh answered, "There are two judges and each of them marks my ride from I to 25 points and marks the steer from I to 25 so the animal you draw makes a big difference."

"So if you and the steer were really good you could get 100 points," Clayton calculated.

Josh laughed. "Well, that's the maximum possible but usually a score in the 70's is pretty good and anything in the 80's is outstanding. Doug Vold marked a 95 in Saddle Bronc at Meadow Lake, Saskatchewan a few years back and Cody Snyder had a 95 in Bull Riding at the Canadian Finals in Edmonton a couple of years ago. Those are about the highest scores ever in Canada, and they were pretty exceptional."

"Well, good luck," Clayton said as he started off.

"Thanks, thanks a lot, Clayton," Josh replied. "By the way, how are you enjoying the rodeo?"

Clayton suddenly realized that he had begun to let his excitement show. Turning away from his cousin, he shrugged, and said over his shoulder, "It's all right. Beats doing homework, I guess." At that the Toronto youngster started off and, as he turned, almost ran smack into his Uncle Roy who was carrying a tray of Cokes.

"Oh, there you are," Roy said, offering each of the boys one of the drinks. "By the way, Clayton, how would you like to sit up in the announcer's stand for the second half of the show? You can see pretty good from up there. I talked to Hank Parker and he said he wouldn't mind a bit."

This time Clayton was careful not to show his elation. He looked down, kicked some dirt and mumbled, "Yeah, that'd be okay." As Clayton followed his uncle towards the announcer's stand, he remembered the scene he had witnessed earlier and decided to ask about it. "What was the excitement before the rodeo?" he queried. "I saw you and Ben take off like you were shot out of a cannon."

"Oh, that," Uncle Roy nodded grimly. "It seems that somebody had an idea about tampering with the stock. But we were lucky, there wasn't any harm done this time."

"What do you mean `tampering with the stock'?" Clayton asked.

They had arrived at the foot of the stairs leading up to the announcer's stand and Roy pointed up the stairs. "I'll tell you all about it later, Clayton," he said. "In the meantime, get on up there and enjoy the rest of the rodeo. I'd better get back to work."

Minutes later he was perched above the chutes and alongside Hank Parker, a genial, heavy-set man who seemed to be forever rustling through notes as he announced the action in the arena to the crowd.

The Calf Roping proved to be a precision event with cowboys competing against the clock as well as each other in an effort to catch, rope and tie the speedy, unwilling, and uncooperative calves. Then, from directly below, Clayton heard his uncle's call to the boys' steer riders. "All right boys, get those ropes on, it's time to rodeo."

Clayton leaned forward as first one boy, then another came out of the chutes, intent on hanging on for eight seconds. Josh was the last rider out and when it came his turn, seven boys had already gone; four had ridden, three had fallen off, and the top score to that point was 70 points.

When Clayton heard Hank Parker telling the crowd that Josh would be coming out of chute number five, he strained forward even harder. He could see his cousin making adjustments to the rope that went around the steer. He watched as Josh got his hand tightly bound into the bull-rope. He saw Josh clench his teeth and nod his head. The gate opened and he was in the arena. The steer leaped high, then kicked out its hind legs, gyrating, twisting, and turning every second. Josh stuck like glue through the early going. A mental clock was ticking off the seconds in Clayton's head. Four seconds. Five seconds.

"Just a little longer," Clayton whispered through his teeth.

Then the steer turned almost completely back towards the chute during one jump. The one hundred and eighty degree move put Josh over to one side and in danger of falling off on the animal's next jump. Josh strained every muscle in his body and forced his way back up into the middle of the steer's back. An instant later, when the horn sounded, he was perfectly astride the hard-bucking steer. As soon as he heard the horn, he leaped from the animal's back and landed easily on the deep dirt floor of the arena.

"How about that!" Announcer Hank Parker shouted into the microphone to the crowd that was already showing its approval of the ride.

"Yeah, how about that!" echoed Clayton in a hushed voice that barely masked his excitement.

Now came the tough part—the wait to find out how Josh scored. The judges would tabulate their marks, the two would be added together and the score would be relayed to Hank Parker who in turn would inform the crowd. The tension mounted and it seemed that everyone was waiting to see if Josh had scored enough points to take the lead. It was a good ride. Even Clayton's inexperienced eye could see that. Had it been good enough?

Then Hank Parker leaned toward his microphone. "All right, ladies and gentlemen, we've got the score on the last cowboy and we've got ourselves a new leader. 73 points for Josh Douglas."

The Steer Riding was over and Clayton descended from the announcer's stand to the area behind the chutes. Josh was receiving the congratulations of the other cowboys.

"That was pretty good," Clayton murmured, watching Josh removing his chaps.

"Thanks, Clayton," his cousin grinned, "I had a real good steer; he really bucked."

"Do you get a trophy now, or what?" Clayton asked.

"Not yet," Josh replied, "maybe not at all. There are two more performances with different guys riding each night. If somebody beats me, there's nothing I can do about it. You only get one chance. Anyway, it's nice to be leading after the first day."

In the background the boys could hear the reaction of the crowd as it was being entertained by the zany antics of a rodeo clown called Tub Willoughby. The crowd was in stitches as the stocky little man in outlandish clothes and makeup tried to extricate himself from the grasp of a female dummy that apparently couldn't resist his charms.

"Come on," Josh urged, "as soon as Tub's act is over it's time for the Bull Riding and there's one ride I don't want to miss!"

"Oh, you mean Lefty Shivers on Bad Medicine?" Clayton remarked casually, remembering his Uncle Roy's conversation with Ben.

"Hey," exclaimed Josh in genuine surprise,

"you're really getting into this, aren't you!"

"Like I said, it beats doing homework," was the answer.

"Let's go then," Josh repeated, "You're not going to find anything like Bull Riding in your algebra book, that's for sure."

John T. Duffy
'87

Chapter Five

The boys found themselves a spot on the walkway behind the chutes, right next to the chute where Lefty Shivers was easing down onto the back of Bad Medicine, a huge, black bull with wide, menacing horns. Lefty, true to his reputation, looked very cocky as he made his final preparations.

"This is a strange bull," Josh explained to Clayton. "He's as docile as a camp dog in the corral and even in the chute. See how he just stands quiet while the cowboy gets ready. But just wait until they open that gate. Then it's a different story."

Clayton heard Hank Parker telling the crowd that Bad Medicine had never been ridden. Lefty turned his head toward the announcer and yelled, "Not `till now, Mister, not `till now."

"Is it okay to cheer for the bull?" Clayton whispered to Josh.

"It sure is when you're part of the stock contractor's family," his cousin answered.

Suddenly there was an explosion of action. The gate opened and Clayton was amazed as the bull's first jump was higher than the top of the chutes. When the bull's front feet hit the ground, his back legs went high in the air. Another jump almost as high as the first followed, this time with a twisting motion thrown in, and, as quickly as it had started, the ride ended. The second time Bad Medicine came down, Lefty Shivers didn't, at least not right away. And when he did, it was a long way from the bull. Clayton was about to let out a whoop, but thought better of the idea.

From the arena, the two boys heard Roy Douglas holler, "Short ride but a good one, Lefty. Must have been one and a half seconds, easy."

"He might've won this round, Douglas," growled the bull rider as he dusted off a shirt that was only slightly less gaudy than that of rodeo clown Tub Willoughby. "But well meet again, and when we do, you'll be laughing out of the other side of your face."

"Lookin' forward to it," Roy answered, his features spread in a wide grin.

The rest of the rodeo performance went smoothly. There was plenty of work to do afterwards but it wasn't long before the stock had all been watered and fed, the equipment put away and it was time to relax. The campers were parked in an open area ringed with cotoonwood trees across from the arena. It was a warm evening, and almost everyone was outside. Ben Bradley and Hank Parker were sitting in lawn chairs next to the Douglas camper, swapping rodeo stories. Laura and Roy were inside putting together a massive platter of sandwiches. Josh was coaching Clayton on throwing a rope, using a straw bale as a target.

The McKannins were camped across from the Douglas camper. Like most of the people involved with the rodeo, they too were enjoying the night air from lawn chairs. Jenny was there too, sitting next to her friend Cindy, and both were watching the two youthful ropers tossing loops hopefully at the bale. Clayton, for his part, stole a number of furtive looks at the two girls seated across the way, but decided to show little interest either in them or the pointers Josh was attempting to pass on. But try as he might to hide it, Clayton's interest in rodeo was growing minute by minute and he kept one ear on the conversation of Ben and Hank, hoping to learn a little more about the sport.

Ben was speaking. "I'm telling you, Hank, the greatest bronc ride I ever saw was Casey Tibbs at the Calgary Stampede. It was when they had the old grandstand, must've been about `57 or `58. I was standing right at the fence, straight out from the chutes. The horse bucked straight toward me and every jump, I mean every jump, I could see daylight between the seat of Casey's pants and the saddle. And spur! I never seen anything like it. His spurs were right over the top of that horse's mane. I'll never forget it as long as I live."

It was the kind of story the older cowboys loved to tell, and the ride always got better with every telling.

Roy emerged from the camper and was about to reply when a commotion started a little way off. It seemed to be coming toward them. Suddenly, a very agitated cowboy burst around the corner of the camper, hollering, cursing and obviously plenty mad.

"What's the matter, Phil?" Roy set down a plate of sandwiches.

"Somebody stole my horse," the angry cowboy fumed. "I ain't joking, Roy. There's a horse thief operating around here."

"That's Phil Streeter. He's a calf roper, a pretty good one too," Josh whispered to Clayton.

"Take it easy a minute," Roy said quietly, "and tell us what happened."

"I already told you what happened," Streeter answered. "I'm supposed to rope tomorrow and somebody got my horse."

"Maybe it wasn't stolen. Maybe he broke his shank and ran off," Ben offered.

"Or maybe a kid just didn't know better and took him for a ride," Hank Parker suggested.

"No way." Streeter shook his head. "I hadn't even got him out of the trailer yet. I just pulled in, went to get a bucket of water and when I came back he was gone."

"That sounds strange all right," Roy agreed. "We better organize a search right now. Josh and Clayton, I want you boys to scout the area on foot. Take flashlights, it'll be dark soon. You think you'd know Phil's horse if you saw him, Josh?"

"I think so Dad," the boy replied. "He's a big appaloosa, isn't he, Phil?"

Phil Streeter nodded glumly.

"Don't worry, Phil, we'll get you mounted on somebody's horse so you can rope tomorrow," Roy encouraged. "In the meantime, maybe we can turn him up tonight. Everybody take your trucks and head a different way out of town. Stop any horse trailers you see and ask if you can have a look. People with nothing to hide won't object. Hank, you go and notify the R.C.M.P. in town. Maybe they'll have some ideas."

In a few minutes a full-scale search was underway. Clayton and Josh paused just long enough to fill their pockets with sandwiches. Jenny and Cindy jumped into the McKannin pickup and with Mr. McKannin at the wheel, they headed for the north road out of town. In a minute the camping area was nearly deserted.

It was close to midnight by the time everyone had returned to the rodeo grounds. The search had turned up no sign of the missing horse or the possible thief. The weary searchers gathered in the Douglas camper over cups of steaming coffee and hot chocolate to review their futile search.

"Looks like a horse thief all right," Ben noted, shaking his head in disgust.

"My guess is that it was somebody not connected with the rodeo. I can't believe a rodeo cowboy would steal another contestant's horse," Phil Streeter put in.

"Maybe it was a prank; somebody playing a practical joke, and the horse will be returned before the rodeo tomorrow," Hank Parker speculated.

"Maybe," Roy replied, "but if he isn't returned, you better make an announcement tomorrow at the rodeo. Maybe somebody in the crowd might have seen something that will give us a clue."

"You bet," Hank agreed.

Ben was rubbing his jaw thoughtfully. "You know," he spoke softly, "it's been a strange year. There's been more incidents of broken and missing equipment, guys being late for rodeos with vehicle breakdowns, horses being sick on the day of a rodeo, and now this. And it seems it's the calf roping event that's been having most of the bad luck. Sure is a strange coincidence," he added.

Roy took a long, slow drink of his coffee, and wondered out loud, "Maybe it's not a coincidence at all."

"You think there could be any connection between this and the little discovery I made earlier, Roy?" Ben asked.

"I'm not sure," Roy shook his head slowly.

"What little discovery?" Josh asked.

"It's what I started telling Clayton about earlier," Roy replied. "Just before the rodeo tonight, Ben found a hypodermic needle on the ground in the pen holding the bulls."

"A needle!" Jenny's high pitched voice repeated.

"It was still full and it's my guess somebody was planning to inject one or more of the bulls and was surprised before he could get it done," said Roy.

"But what for?" It was Clayton's turn to speak.

"I'm not sure, Clayton," his uncle answered. "But I'm guessing that there's a sedative in the syringe and the idea was to sedate some of the bulls to keep them from bucking very hard."

"So the cowboys could ride them?" Clayton wondered aloud.

"Maybe, but that wouldn't make much sense," Roy replied. "A cowboy can't make any money on an animal that doesn't buck, even if he does ride him."

"Then what's the reason for it, Dad?" asked Josh.

"The only thing I can figure is that somebody is out to make us look bad," Roy replied. "If we put on a bad show, we could lose some rodeos and if we lose very many rodeos, we'd soon be out of business."

"But who would want to see you out of business, Roy?" asked Ben. "Heck, your rodeos are as good as any in the country."

"I bet I know the answer to that." Jenny jumped up from her chair. "It's those Shivers boys. None of 'em are any good. Didn't they try to buy our outfit a couple of years ago? They didn't even offer a fair price! They're probably behind all the rotten things that have been happening to us lately. I bet they figure they can force us out of business and get the D Lazy D for practically nothin'." She sat down and crossed her arms to emphasize her point.

"Now hold on there, Jen," Roy spoke patiently. "Let's not be jumping to conclusions. We don't have any proof who's behind this and until we do I don't want anybody making any wild accusations."

"One thing I don't understand," Clayton looked at his uncle. "How would stealing Phil Streeter's calf-roping horse hurt the D Lazy D?"

"Good question, Clayton," Roy replied. "I can't see how it would, which means that the two sets of incidents could be unrelated. And that makes the whole mystery even harder to figure." He stood up and drank the last of his coffee. "On that note, I think we better be turning in. We've got another rodeo tomorrow."

Clayton had trouble sleeping that night as his mind wrestled with the mystery that had suddenly confronted the rodeo. It had been a full day and every time he closed his eyes, Clayton could see pictures of all he had encountered. He thought of the colourful Grand Entry that had begun the rodeo. He thought about Josh's ride. For a while, he even mentally rehearsed throwing a rope as Josh had shown him.

But always his thoughts returned to the mysterious happenings of the rodeo. What was the meaning of the hypodermic needle Ben and Uncle Roy had found? Was the theft of Phil Streeter's horse an isolated incident or part of a series of events? If it was a series of events, what could be the reason? And, who was the culprit? Was the same person responsible for the misfortunes that had been plaguing the D Lazy D?

Chapter Six

The remaining two performances at the Taber rodeo were relatively uneventful. On the final day the next-to-last boys' steer rider marked a 74 so Josh had to settle for second place. But he was still happy. The second-place prize money put him in fifth place overall in the season standings. That meant he would be eligible for the Calgary Stampede. Not only that but if he were able to maintain his position for the whole year, Josh would be among the six steer riders competing in the Canadian Finals Rodeo in November.

The rodeo was over and the job of cleaning up and preparing to move back home was underway. Roy and Ben were loading the stock into the liners. The cowboys and cowgirls who had won in Taber were picking up their prize money. Those who hadn't were putting their equipment into pickup trucks, vans and campers and getting ready to head either back home or on to the next rodeo.

Clayton was helping Josh clean tack and return it to the Douglas tack trailer when two boys approached them.

"Hey, Douglas," one of them yelled unpleasantly, "I hear you won second here."

"That's right, Miles," Josh replied. Clayton turned and studied the two boys. They were both bigger than himself and Josh, and both looked like they had just been dragged down a dusty road. Their clothes were only slightly dirtier than their faces. The boy who had spoken to Josh was huskier than his companion and neither of them looked particularly friendly.

"I suppose you probably drew the best steer again, eh, Douglas? Seems like that always happens

48

at one of your old man's rodeos," the boy called Miles continued.

Josh stood up and faced him. "You know better than that," he said, anger rising in his voice. "Dad had nothing to do with the draw."

"Yeah, well, it seems funny to me that at every Douglas rodeo I get a steer that doesn't buck and you seem to draw real good," the bigger boy retorted.

"Look, we've got work to do. If you've said your piece, why don't you run along and do your whining somewhere else," Josh told him.

"Who's your friend, Douglas?" Miles sneered.

"He's my cousin from Toronto, Clayton Findlay." Turning back to his work, Josh spoke to Clayton, ignoring the pair behind them. "The mouthy one's Miles Shivers, Lefty's little brother; you'll notice the resemblance. The other one's Clint Runner."

It wasn't an introduction so Clayton didn't bother to say hello to the two arrivals, one of whom he had already developed a strong dislike for.

Miles Shivers wasn't finished. "There's a lot of people saying D Lazy D stock isn't good enough for a professional circuit," he said.

"I doubt if anybody has said anything like that, except for you and your brother maybe," Josh said as he turned back toward the antagonist.

"It's true, Douglas," Miles Shivers went on, "everybody's sayin' it's just a matter of time until the Douglas rodeo string is out of business. It's about time too. Those carcasses you're packin' are sorry excuses for bucking horses and bulls."

"You mean like Bad Medicine," Clayton interjected. The comment was so sudden and unexpected that Josh laughed out loud.

"Yeah, now there's a carcass," he added. "Just think how fast he would have put Lefty on the ground if he could really buck."

"My brother'll ride that bull next time. That is, if your old man doesn't rig the draw to see that Lefty never gets him again," Miles Shivers sneered.

Josh wasn't laughing now. "My dad doesn't rig the draw and you know it, Miles," he said quietly.

"Don't upset yourself, Douglas," was the reply. "I'd probably be a little touchy, too, if my old man was just about finished and was using any little tricks he could to hang on."

That was too much for Josh and without warning he hurled himself at his adversary. The two fell to the ground, rolling and throwing punches although neither was landing any telling blows. They struggled to their feet again and for a moment stood, each with his arms locked around the other, both of them straining and grunting. Although Miles probably outweighed Josh by twenty pounds, for a while there seemed to be no advantage on the part of either fighter.

Then, just as it appeared that Josh might be getting the upper hand, he was tripped by Clint Runner who, until that point, had played no part in the argument or the fight. Without hesitation, Clayton lowered his head and charged the second youth. He heard a groan as the wind whooshed out of his opponent from the force of the tackle.

The fortunes were quickly reversed, however, as Clint Runner was bigger, stronger, and probably more used to mixing it up than Clayton. In a moment Clayton was on the receiving end of a pretty fair pounding, but he showed no sign of either giving in or displaying any fear. Instead, he redoubled his efforts and was giving a gritty account of himself in spite of the odds.

It was at this moment that Clayton felt a powerful hand take the back of his shirt and yank him back. A big, suntanned cowboy in an expensive-looking blazer stepped between him and Clint Runner. "That'll do, men," the newcomer said firmly although Clayton thought he detected a hint of a smile on the man's face. "That's enough fightin' for today," he repeated as he separated the other two combatants.

Josh was sporting a cut on his upper lip and Miles Shivers had a bruise above his cheek that looked like it had the makings of a pretty fair shiner.

"I haven't seen so many fists flyin' since the last time I was at a rodeo dance and all the pretty women were fightin' over me," the stranger laughed, keeping himself between the four adversaries.

"I'll be seeing you again, Douglas, and your cousin, too," Miles Shivers snarled as he turned and walked away. Clint Runner followed him.

"Cousin, eh," the peacemaker eyed Clayton. "I would have said you were kin to a wildcat of some description the way you were scrappin'."

"How are you, Len?" Josh said to the man between gulps of air as he tried to catch his breath. "By the way, meet my cousin Clayton. Clayton, this is Len Tucker."

"Howdy, Clayton, pleased to meet you," Len Tucker grinned as he shook the boy's hand. "Where's that grouchy pa of yours hangin' out? I came by to swap a few lies with him," he said to Josh.

"Dad should be back any minute, Len," Josh answered.

Clayton found himself liking Len Tucker, with his ever present grin and ready wit. He looked to be about the same age as Uncle Roy, though not quite as big. Clayton was about to ask him if he was a contestant when his uncle came around the corner with Ben. Len Tucker exchanged greetings with Roy and Ben, and then Roy noticed his son's split lip.

"What happened to you?" he demanded, "You weren't fighting were you?"

"No, they weren't fightin'," Len Tucker interjected with a wink at the boys. "As a matter of fact, Roy, just as I came along, I saw these two young men chasin' down a runaway horse with a woman on it screamin' for dear life. It was awful! She was tryin' to hold on to a little baby and get that horse under control at the same time. Or was it two babies?" he looked at Clayton as if for confirmation.

"That's right," Len resumed in mock seriousness, "it was two babies, and she had a box of Kentucky fried chicken, too. And she was screamin', and the babies were crying', and chicken was spillin' and the horse was runnin', and if it wasn't for these two boys jumpin' in and gettin' that horse stopped, there's no tellin' what might've happened."

By the end of Len Tucker's far-fetched explanation, Josh and Clayton were both laughing but they became serious when Roy asked, "Who were you fighting with?"

"Miles Shivers," Josh replied, his head down.

"You know I don't like fighting," his father stated. "Was there a good reason for it?"

"I guess not," Josh mumbled in reply.

52

"Yes, there was," Clayton spoke up. "He said you rigged the draw so Josh would win, and he said your stock wasn't good enough and he said you were just about finished in the rodeo business and he said that…"

"Hold on there," Roy interrupted, a slow smile coming over his features, "I think I get the idea. Judging from the looks of you, it appears you got into the action too," he observed.

"Clint Runner tried to make it an unfair fight and Clayton helped me out," Josh was quick to point out.

"Well, see if you two can stay out of trouble for a while. We'll be ready to leave soon," Roy said, with no hint of anger in his voice.

"None of that's true, Roy," Len Tucker was speaking again, "I tell you it was a runaway horse. Come to think of it, I think that poor woman had three babies."

"Shut up, Len," Roy laughed, "and get over here and have a cup of coffee. I see you won a little money here."

"Yeah, I managed a third in the Calf Roping but I got tossed off another one of your bulls. Oh well, I guess I made enough to keep the wolves away from the door for another week."

The men sat down as Ben fetched the coffee from the camper and poured three cups. For a while they drank in silence, each man immersed in his own thoughts.

"It was nice of you to mount Phil Streeter on your horse," Ben finally said.

"Didn't do him much good," Len Tucker shrugged. "But you know what it's like roping off a strange horse. Tough break for him, somebody making off with his horse like that. What do you fellas make of it?"

"I don't know what to think, Len," Roy began, "but I don't like it. We've never had anything like this in rodeo before and we don't need it now. If it was an isolated incident, I wouldn't be as worried, but there've been just too many unexplained accidents and mishaps. It's serious, that's for sure."

"You're right. I sure can't figure it out," Len agreed. "I guess all we can do is keep our eyes peeled for any strange goings-on."

"I don't know what else can be done for the time being," Roy concurred.

The three cowboys chatted a while longer and Len Tucker stood up. "Well, thanks for the coffee. I know you fellas have to hit the road, so I'll be moving along. So long, Josh. See ya, Wildcat," Len grinned at Clayton and with a wave headed off into the darkness that was beginning to fall over the campground.

Ben and Roy busied themselves readying the vehicles for the trip back to the D Lazy D and Josh and Clayton were left alone.

"I wanted to thank you for helping me out in the scrap," Josh told his cousin.

"That's okay. I couldn't stand by and watch you take on two of them, could I?" Clayton answered.

"It's funny, Clint Runner isn't really a bad guy but when he's around Miles, he doesn't seem like the same kid," Josh murmured.

"Runner, that's a different kind of name," Clayton commented.

"It's an Indian name," Josh told him. "Clint comes from the Stoney Reserve out by Morley. That's not very far from our place. Like I said, he's not really a bad guy, but he's kind of shy and he doesn't have too many friends in rodeo. It's too bad he had to fall in with a snake like Miles Shivers."

"I think I can understand why Jenny got so fired up talking about the Shivers boys," Clayton observed. "They're easy not to like."

"Yeah, this is one time I have to agree with my sister," Josh nodded.

"Len Tucker seems like an all right guy." Clayton couldn't help but laugh as he recalled the cowboy's wildly fabricated story.

"You bet he is," Josh confirmed. "One of the best. He's been around a long time. You know he's been trying to win the All-Round Championship of Canada for as long as I can remember. He's been second four times but he's never quite made it to the top. It must be frustrating for him and yet he's always the same way, laughing and joking every time you see him."

"What's an All-Round championship?" Clayton asked.

"It's sort of like the name sounds. It's the one championship every cowboy would like to win. To qualify, a contestant has to compete in both a riding event and a timed event. Len ropes calves and rides bulls so he qualifies. The guy who wins the most in his combined events over the whole year is the champion," Josh explained.

"You mean everybody doesn't go in every event?"

"No, actually most guys specialize in one event," Josh went on. "There are only a few who compete in two or more events and even fewer who work a timed event and a riding event. Now Lefty Shivers is a guy who works three events, Calf Roping, Saddle

Bronc and Bull Riding which gives him an advantage over somebody like Len who only works two."

Clayton made a face. "You mean Lefty Shivers could be the All-Round Champion of Canada?"

Josh nodded. "He's the season leader so far. Has a real good chance," he declared. "That's all the more reason why we'd all like to see Len win it."

"Well, maybe this will be his year," Clayton suggested.

"Yeah, that would be nice, but whether he does or doesn't, it won't bother Len any, He'll still be as happy-go-lucky as ever. Hey, we better get moving or they'll be leaving us behind and it's a long walk home," Josh urged, and the two boys gathered up the last of the equipment to be loaded into the camper.

Clayton was quiet and thoughtful as the two boys finished up. When the last piece of equipment was put away, he suddenly grabbed his cousin by the arm. "There's something I better tell you," he said, facing Josh in the twilight. "I helped you out back there because I didn't think two against one was fair. I don't want you to think that because of the fight, I'm suddenly becoming like you and Uncle Roy and all these other cowboys. I still wish I wasn't here, but I'm stuck and I have to make the best of it, that's all. Don't think there's anything more to it than that."

Josh was thunderstruck. Just when it looked as if Clayton was beginning to come around, this latest outburst appeared to contradict everything. Josh was about to reply but he was interrupted by the return of Roy and Ben. Both men seemed agitated.

"Come on, boys, we've got to move out fast," Roy' voice shook with emotion as he spoke. "I just

56

got a call at the rodeo office from one of the hands at home. Doc Holliday's down. The vet's there and he doesn't know what's wrong but it doesn't look good. Let's go!"

Instantly Roy, Ben, and Josh vaulted into the cabs of the two trucks, leaving Clayton standing alone and feeling a pain much greater than that from any of Clint Runner's blows. Here was his trusted friend and confidant, the one thing that really meant something to him in this strange new world, who was about to be lost to him. The animal with whom he shared a strange yet undeniable bond was down. Clayton wasn't even sure what that meant but he knew it had to be serious.

The thought pounded inside him like the clanging of a bell that couldn't be silenced. His legs seemed to move of their own accord as he climbed into the liner with Ben and Josh. The words echoed in his head over and over. Doc Holliday's down. Doc Holliday's down!

Chapter Seven

The drive home was a quiet one. The usually talkative Ben was hunched grimly over the wheel, every fibre in his body bent on getting the mammoth eighteen-wheel truck and liner over the distance to the D Lazy D in as short a time as possible.

Next to him sat Josh, who like Ben, kept his eyes straight ahead, peering into the blackness of the night and the splash of light ahead of them on the highway from the truck's headlights.

Clayton sat by the door, looking out the side window, but seeing nothing. His thoughts were back at the ranch with the horse he had come to care so much about. From time to time, he brushed a sleeve over a moist cheek, but made no attempt to hide his silent tears.

The hours seemed to pass slowly but finally the lights of the ranch became visible in the distance. A few minutes later, both liners had pulled into the yard. Their cabs emptied quickly and the concerned group sprinted to the corral that was the home of Doc Holliday.

Jim Fletcher, the veterinarian, met them at the gate. He addressed Roy. "I've got him in a stall in the barn," he reported. "I'm thinking it's got to be colic, Roy. It's come on fast and I don't think there's a thing we can do. I've made him as comfortable as possible. He's lying down. Probably takes a little of the pressure off. I'd let him do what makes him feel best. Other than that all you can do is wait. I'll give you a call in the morning."

"Thanks a lot, Jim," Roy replied, "I really appreciate your coming out."

Quietly, Roy, Ben, Josh and Clayton entered the

barn and approached the stricken animal's stall. Doc Holliday nickered gently as he recognized the familiar faces, but all four could readily see that the deadly illness had sapped the animal's once mighty strength.

Roy stepped forward and bent over the stallion, his voice low and gentle as he talked to him. Doc Holliday made no move. For a long time the stall was quiet except for the labored breathing of the horse and the even tone of Roy's voice as he ran a hand along the animal's side. After a long time, Roy stood up and turned to the others. His eyes were moist as he said, "We may as well go up to the house. There's nothing more we can do for him. If he isn't any better in the morning I'll have Jim put him down. He's been too good a horse to let him suffer." Roy led the way back to the door of the barn. Ben and Josh fell silently in behind him.

Clayton hesitated a minute, then said, "If it's all right with you, I'll just wait here for a while."

Uncle Roy turned and for a minute debated with himself whether he should leave the boy behind or not. Finally he nodded. "All right, Clayton, but don't stay too long. It still gets pretty chilly at night."

Clayton had already returned to Doc Holliday's stall. By the time the other three had left the barn, the boy was crawling down alongside the jet-black animal. Clayton eased himself into a corner of the stall next to the horse's head. He fastened the top button of his jacket, pulled some loose straw over his legs to ward off the cold and began to talk.

"Well, Doc, you don't have a thing to worry about, because I'm going to stay right here with you just as long as you want. Just you and me boy, we'll sit here till you get better. Heck, 1 don't even know what colic is, but I know it isn't anything that a horse like you and a kid like me can't lick, right?"

He looked around and for a moment was struck by the thought of what his Toronto friends would think, if they could see him huddled in a cold stable next to a wild horse. He smiled at the thought. "Hey, Doc, guess what. I looked in a book about Doc Holliday in the library the other day. I mean the first one, you know? He was a famous outlaw in the Old West. I guess that fits all right because you've been kind of an outlaw too. You ever hear of the O.K. Corral? Well, that's where Doc Holliday got in this famous gunfight. It was him and the Earp Brothers against a bunch of guys who were even worse outlaws than he was."

And so it went. For the rest of that night, the boy from the East who couldn't seem to fit into his new surroundings, sat shivering in a dark straw-covered stall in a damp, cold barn and talked to a dying horse about an outlaw, about Toronto, about his parents and about every dream and hope that had ever filled his young mind. And every once in a while, the boy would stop, sometimes in mid-sentence, to look at the suffering animal beside him and whisper, "I won't leave you, Doc."

Chapter Eight

The first rays of morning sunlight stole through the cracks of the barn's old wooden walls and found their way onto the face of the boy huddled in the corner of the stall. He was fast asleep. His position hadn't changed when, a few minutes later, his Uncle Roy approached the stall. Shaking his head in disbelief, Roy bent down and gently nudged his nephew awake. Clayton woke with a start, and after taking a second or two to get his bearings, turned to where Doc Holliday lay.

The horse didn't appear to have moved much but his eyes were wide open and fixed intently on the boy's face.

Clayton looked from the horse to his uncle. "What do you think?" he asked.

"You spent the night out here, didn't you?" Roy asked him.

Clayton only nodded and his eyes returned to the face of Doc Holliday. "What do you think?" he repeated, "Is he getting any better?"

Roy looked at the horse and ran a hand over the animal's black shoulder. "I don't know, son. I'll say this though, he isn't any worse, so maybe there's still a chance." He hesitated before adding, "Why did you do it, Clayton?"

"I don't know. I guess...well...I guess...because he needs me—and he's the only one who does!" The boy's words suddenly became an angry torrent.

"My parents don't need me. They're off in some other part of the world and they sent me out here to get rid of me for a while. You don't need me here, all I do is mess up things for you and everybody. But this horse," Clayton's voice broke to a whisper, "he needs me, he likes me, he's the only one."

For a while, Roy studied his nephew's defiant face. "So that's it," he breathed, almost to himself. Aloud, he said, "Well, if we're going to save this horse, we've got to get him up. He's got to move around." Roy left the stall and returned seconds later carrying a red halter with a lead shank attached to the end of it. Slowly he approached Doc Holliday. As the horse raised his head uneasily, Roy gently slipped the halter in place.

"Now, Clayton," he said in a low voice, "this is the hard part. First we've got to get him to his feet. I think he might get up for you. But once he's up, be careful. He isn't broke. He's wild and unpredictable. Even though he's sick he may try something out of fear. Do you understand?"

Clayton nodded and eased forward on hands and knees, the straw rustling beneath him as he inched his way closer to the horse. "Okay, now Doc, it's you and me now, nothing to worry about, we're just going to get you up for a walk around. Easy now, easy." Clayton continued to let the horse hear the sound of his voice as he took hold of the halter and rope. "Now, Doc, up you get, come on, I know you can do it," Clayton coaxed and clucked his tongue.

Doc Holliday raised his head for an instant, then gave up and slumped down again. Clayton stroked the top of the animal's head and started again. "That's all right, Doc. Rest up and we'll try it once more. I know you can do it, I know you can. Okay, now, we're gonna do this together, you hear me. I'll stand and you just stand up with me." Clayton paused, took a deep breath and continued, "All right, this is it. Up, Doc. Now. Get up. Come on."

The boy's voice was steady, never wavering as he encouraged the stallion to try one more time. The horse raised his head again and with a mighty thrust got his front legs underneath him. For a moment, Doc Holliday swayed unsteadily and seemed about to lay back down.

Clayton's voice grew sterner. "Come on, Doc. You have to get up. You've got to. Come on, you can do it. Come on. All the way, Doc. Now. NOW!"

With a second mighty heave the horse lurched to his feet. He stood uncertainly, head down, bearing little resemblance to the outlaw that had once put the toughest cowboys on the ground time after time. Finally he brought his head up and shook himself.

Roy backed out of the stall swinging the door open as he moved. "Try and bring him out, Clayton. See if you can get him out into the paddock so we can walk him around, but if he acts up, drop the shank and get out of his way," he instructed.

Again Clayton coaxed and the horse followed, stepping gingerly at first, as if to test untrustworthy legs. Slowly and carefully the unlikely pair moved through the barn and out into the paddock. Roy followed behind. Once outside, Roy told Clayton, "Keep him moving if you can. Try not to let him stop even if he wants to."

Clayton began the walk round and round the paddock, slowly and steadily tracing and retracing a path around the outer perimeter. He walked at the horse's head with one hand on the lead rope and the other on the halter. On the few occasions when the boy spoke, it was to the horse and his voice was barely audible.

Roy retired to the fence and assumed a perch on the top rail in order to watch his nephew and the horse in their determined, almost rhythmic march. After several minutes had gone by, Josh appeared at the corral, slipped through the rails of the fence and fell in alongside his cousin. After a long passage of time during which neither had spoken, Josh finally said simply, "You're wrong, you know."

"What?" asked Clayton.

"What you said before about not being needed and wanted, you're wrong about that."

"How did you..." Clayton began.

"I was in the barn," Josh told him. "I heard you talking to Dad and I figured you wouldn't want me around. So I snuck out without you seeing me," He pulled a couple of slightly battered cookies from his jeans pocket and offered one to Clayton. For the first time, Clayton was aware of the gnawing in his stomach. He accepted the food gratefully but without comment.

Between bites Josh said, "If he lives, it'll be because of you."

Clayton shook his head at the statement.

"It's true," Josh insisted, "none of us stayed with him all night, and it probably wouldn't have done any good if we had. Likely would have made him jumpy and worse in the long run."

"You're just sayin' that," Clayton answered, looking hard at his cousin.

"No, I'm not," came the reply. "And another thing, where do you think my Dad would be without Doc? I'll tell you where. Without his colts, it wouldn't be long before our string would be like Miles Shivers said it is. We need him. You were right about one thing though," Josh continued. "Doc needed you. He needed you to save his life. But we need you too. That's the part you're wrong about."

Both boys fell silent, apparently lost in thought, and for several minutes the only sounds were the soft footfalls of the two cousins and the steady, uninterrupted cadence of Doc Holliday's hooves behind them. When conversation resumed, it was Clayton who spoke. "You wouldn't happen to have any more of those cookies, would you?" he asked.

"Yeah, as a matter of fact, I do," Josh answered as his hand fished in another pocket and emerged with two more of the crumbling, out-of-shape lumps.

This time Clayton grinned his appreciation and said, "Thanks, Josh, thanks a lot." He devoured the cookie hungrily, passed a shirt-sleeve carelessly over his mouth and turning to Josh, said, "Look, I just want you to know. I didn't mean what I said after the fight. The truth is...well, I was glad to help you."

"I'm awful glad you did," Josh smiled at his cousin, then with a straight face added, "But what fight are you talking about? I thought we saved a lady and some kids on a runaway horse."

"And don't forget the box of chicken," Clayton laughed at the memory. The two boys' laughter sealed their long-delayed friendship and the conversation that followed was no different from that of any other two teenagers with much to share.

Almost two hours had passed when Roy jumped down from the fence and called, "I think you can take that halter off your horse now, Clayton. Looks like he's moving pretty good now."

Clayton started removing the halter, then stopped suddenly. "What did you say?" he asked.

"I said, go ahead and take the halter off him," Roy replied.

"No, the other part," Clayton repeated. "The other part of what you said."

"Oh," Roy tried to resist a smile as he said, "You mean the part about *your* horse? That part?"

"Uncle Roy, you don't really mean that, do you?" Clayton was incredulous.

"As a matter of fact, I do, son," came the reply. "You see, this horse never really belonged to me. Oh, he's lived here on the D Lazy D and he's eaten my feed, and kicked down a few of my fence rails and given me some good-looking colt prospects. But he's never belonged to me, or any other man for that matter. Not till now that is. Now if it's all right with you, I'd like to borrow your horse from time to time to keep those colts coming along, but if ever I saw a man and a horse that belonged to each other, you two are it."

At that, Clayton flipped the halter from Doc's head, and with a whoop the horse and his new owner were running for the far end of the corral, leaving Roy and Josh standing together.

"Do you think Doc's going to make it, Dad?" Josh asked.

"You know something," the stock contractor smiled down at his son, "I think they're both going to make it."

Chapter Nine

Clayton was puzzled. The one-time city boy was becoming as western as if he'd been born and raised on the ranch, and the realization caught him by surprise. He still thought often and fondly of Toronto, particularly those things about the city he loved most: the Blue Jays, the new-wave look of Queen Street West with its artists' quarter, the streetcars, the ethnic flavour of Kensington market, the frequent family visits to Toronto Island and, most of all, the architecture.

For as long as he could remember, Clayton had wanted to be an architect. To a boy with that goal, Toronto's varied cityscape was paradise. Few cities combined, as that one did, the old — as in the quaintness of some of the Victorian style houses and the stateliness of the University of Toronto campus, and the modern — from the science-fiction style city hall to that most striking of all Toronto landmarks, the 1800 foot-high CN Tower.

And Clayton loved all of it. Yet here he was, well on his way to becoming, of all things...a cowboy. And enjoying it! Yet what else could he do, he reasoned. Here he was, living on a ranch in the Alberta foothills, travelling the rodeo circuit and now — the owner of his own horse.

His Uncle Roy's pronouncement that Doc Holliday was to be his was exactly what had been needed to complete the transition. After all, architecture would always be there, but for now, Clayton was content to follow a way of life he had never even considered before. Clayton Findlay was a cowboy.

The next days were especially exciting for the west's most recent convert. He was up at sunup and out to the corral to groom the recuperating Doc Holliday. Then a quick feed of hay and oats for the horse and Clayton had to rush back into the house for his own breakfast before sprinting out the door and out to the gate to await the arrival of the school bus.

No longer did Clayton dread the mealtime gatherings in the Douglas kitchen. Even Jenny's most acidic barbs received only grins or good-natured kidding in return. Jenny had been very put-out at having missed a lot of the action. She and Cindy McKannin had been cooling down their barrel racing horses and missed Josh and Clayton's fight at Taber. Then, because she was travelling with the McKannins, she had not known about the drama centered around Doc Holliday's nearly fatal illness and the subsequent bond that had been formed between the horse and her eastern cousin.

Although she was reluctant to admit it, the sometimes brash cowgirl was slowly changing her opinion about Clayton. Jenny was first and foremost an animal lover and anyone willing to show the kind of devotion to an animal that Clayton had shown with the ailing Doc Holliday was sure to win her admiration, grudging though it was. Furthermore, Jenny, for all her temper tantrums and cantankerousness, was unfailingly loyal and devoted to her twin brother. To Jenny, willingness to fight alongside Josh meant that her cousin was now an ally. It was as simple as that. Then too, she had been impressed by Clayton's ability to give as good as he got in the practical jokes department. A scrapper herself, she admired the quality in others.

It wasn't long, in spite of her efforts not to allow that admiration to show, that her true feelings came out. It was during the evening meal a few days later that her changed attitude first became evident. The conversation had come around to whether or not Clayton would be allowed to try to break and ride Doc Holliday. Uncle Roy and Aunt Laura opposed the idea.

"This horse was never broke to ride, Clayton," Roy reasoned. "He was a bucking horse and one of the toughest there ever was. He was halter-broke as a colt so he can be led. But leading a horse around a corral and riding it are very different."

"Especially with a horse of his temperament," Aunt Laura added.

"But he trusts me," Clayton argued. "I don't believe he'd do anything to hurt me."

"Maybe so, Clayton," Roy countered. "But this horse spent nine years pitching cowboys on the ground. It's in his blood. When someone gets on his back, his natural response is to get that person off. It has nothing to do with wanting to hurt anybody."

"Dad's right, Clayton," Josh added between mouthfuls. "I know how you feel about Doc and I can't blame you for wanting to try but I think it'd be way too dangerous."

"Beans!" exploded Jenny, who to this point had listened in silence. "I think you should let him try. What's the use of having a horse of your own if you can't ride him?"

Roy looked steadily at his daughter. "I know Jen, but you've got to remember that Clayton hasn't had much experience with horses and breaking this horse would take an expert."

"That's right," came the defiant reply. "That's why I'm going to help him."

"Y...You," sputtered Josh. "But I thought you couldn't stand..." He caught himself just in time.

"Dad, you've always said I'm the best hand around horses you've ever seen," Jenny charged on immodestly. "If you meant that and if you really want Clayton to have a horse of his own, then you'll let us try."

Jenny had a point. Even at her tender years, she was considered to be an expert horsewoman. In particular, her ability to gentle ill-mannered horses was known far beyond the confines of her own family.

"But we have so many horses," Aunt Laura pointed out. "Clayton, you could have your pick."

The boy shook his head stubbornly. Perhaps some of Jenny's headstrong ways were beginning to rub off. "Doc's my horse," he countered. "Uncle Roy, you said so yourself. You should at least give me a chance."

There was a long interval of silence broken only by sounds of cutlery on plates and slow, deliberate chewing.

Finally Roy put down his knife and fork, wiped at the corners of his mouth with his napkin and looked long and hard at his nephew. "All right, you can try," he capitulated. "But, there are two conditions. You must never work with him when you're alone. One of us," here he paused and glanced at his daughter whose eyes were wide with anticipation, "preferably Jenny, has to be there at all times."

"All right!" Jenny rejoiced.

"Secondly," Roy went on, "the first time he throws you, that's it. End of experiment. Do you understand?"

"If he throws me," Clayton amended.

"If he throws you," his uncle added with a smile.

With that Clayton let out a holler and bolted from the table and out the door. He wanted to let Doc Holliday in on the news without delay.

At the dinner table meanwhile, all eyes were directed at Jenny. For her part, the unpredictable teenager was concentrating on a second slice of pot roast as if nothing at all had happened. Josh could contain himself no longer. "I don't get it," he told her. "I was convinced you didn't like Clayton. You've been treating him like he was from another planet. So why the sudden change?"

Jenny studied her fork in silence, but a mischievous look in her eye gave her away. "Dad always says females change their minds," she pointed out. "Well, I'm female and I guess I just changed mine."

The four Douglases dissolved into laughter and launched into second helpings. Not far away, in a circular corral, a boy was animatedly passing on big news to his best friend.

Chapter Ten

The work with Doc Holliday would have to wait a few days. Roy wanted to be certain the horse had made a complete recovery. Besides, the weekend was coming up and weekends meant rodeos. This was one of the rare times during the year that the Douglas outfit was not contracted to be at a rodeo, but that wouldn't stop Josh and Jenny from hitting the road to compete.

The McKannins were planning to take Cindy to weekend competitions in Brooks, Alberta and Great Falls, Montana and were most willing to take the neighbor youngsters along. More than once, Cindy had been given the same courtesy by the Douglases. In fact, throughout the close-knit rodeo fraternity, cowboys caught rides with other cowboys whenever possible. Young competitors often travelled with the families of fellow competitors in order to make the endless hours on the road a little easier and more economical.

Roy and Laura Douglas welcomed the respite from the hectic rodeo schedule. There was plenty of work to be done around the D Lazy D and seldom was there enough time to do it. The McKannins would be picking up Josh and Jenny early Saturday morning, so Friday evening was spent in preparation. The Douglas living room was a beehive of activity. Jenny spent the time sorting her tack and packing for the impending trip while Josh made adjustments to his spurs and bull rope. Clayton was sprawled on the floor surrounded by books on the subject of breaking horses. He was a little disappointed at not being able to go along but was determined to put the time to good use by learning all he could about horses and breaking them to ride. Occasionally he glanced enviously at his two cousins, but their attention never once deviated from the tasks in front of them. It was as if they had forgotten he was there.

Suddenly, in the middle of applying a coat of oil to her saddle, Jenny asked him sharply, "Well, aren't you planning to take along a change of clothes or anything?"

"What are you talking about?" Clayton demanded. "A change of clothes for what?"

"We're going to be gone for two days and normally people change their clothes in that time," Jenny replied haughtily.

"You mean…" Clayton looked at Josh who was having trouble suppressing a grin. "You mean I'm going along? Really?"

"We asked Mr. McKannin the other day if he had room, and he said `no problem'," Josh laughed. "But Jenny wouldn't let me say anything. She wanted to keep you in suspense."

"It's okay, Uncle Roy?" Clayton looked to his uncle who was reading on the chesterfield. "I mean, don't you need help around here?"

Roy looked up and smiled at the eager youngster. "I imagine your aunt and I will be able to get along for a couple of days." He winked at his wife who had been enjoying the whole scene. "Of course, you'll have to work a little extra hard when you get back," he added with a chuckle.

The next morning Clayton was the first one at the back door. Suitcase in hand, and bedecked in one of Josh's discarded cowboy hats, he was a sharp contrast to the disgruntled young man who had disembarked from the train in Calgary a few short weeks before.

Josh and Jenny made sleepy-eyed appearances a little later—this was, after all, old hat to them. Roy arrived minutes later and announced that no one was going anywhere until breakfast had been dispensed with. Reluctantly, Clayton joined the rest of the Douglas family at the table, but was unable to muster much enthusiasm on this occasion for Corn Flakes and french toast.

Breakfast was barely out of the way when the sound of a horn blast from the yard signalled the arrival of the McKannins. A period of frenzied activity followed as Clayton and Josh loaded suitcases and rodeo equipment into the McKannin camper. Cindy and Jenny ran to a nearby corral to fetch Jenny's barrel-racing horse. Jenny's horse was a smallish mare with a big heart. The girls soon returned with "Sugar" and loaded her alongside Cindy's grey gelding, "Catfish," in the horse trailer behind the truck and camper.

Mr. McKannin and Roy exchanged greetings while Mrs. McKannin ran inside to say hello to Laura. It wasn't long until the caravan was underway and the travellers settled down for the three hour drive to Brooks.

For the first while, Jenny and Cindy chatted away catching up on all the news, which seemed odd to the boys, seeing as they had seen one another as recently as the day before at school.

Josh stared out the window, content to enjoy the passing Alberta scenery. Clayton tried to do the same but found his attention diverted more and more in the direction of Cindy McKannin. He had noticed her before, at the rodeo in Taber, and at school where she was a classmate. But this was the first time he'd been this close to her and he was pleasantly surprised, first at how pretty she was; and secondly at her friendly, bubbly personality.

It wasn't long before the conversation turned to the subject of the mysterious goings-on at recent rodeos. Jenny was first to offer an opinion. "I still say the Shivers boys are behind it all," she stated. "They're a bunch of no-goods, rotten-to-the-core, and everybody knows Lefty wants to get into the stock contracting business. He'd just love to get his hands on the D Lazy D."

"Well, that would explain all the things that have happened to us," Josh mused thoughtfully. "But what about at the rodeos themselves, like Phil Streeter's horse disappearing. It doesn't add up."

"Wait a minute," Clayton interjected. "What do you mean 'all the things that have happened to us'? I heard something about that before but nobody's ever really explained."

"Well," Josh started slowly. "It all started about a year ago. Little things like the stock not performing like they should at a few rodeos. Dad had them checked out and it seemed they got into some bad feed. Not bad enough to kill them, just put them off a little, so they wouldn't buck like they can."

"The funny part is," Jenny picked up the story, "we do all our own feeding at every rodeo we go to. Dad had our feed checked and there was nothing wrong with it. So that means..." she paused.

"Somebody must have tampered with it," Clayton filled in the answer.

"Right," agreed Josh.

"Then there was the accident with the liner," Jenny added.

"That was a close call," Josh noted. "We were taking stock to Edmonton for the Canadian Finals

Rodeo last November. The brakes failed on one of the liners and it went in the ditch and rolled."

"Geez, you're kidding!" Clayton was flabbergasted. "That must have been awful."

"We were lucky," Jenny added. "Ben was driving and when he realized he had no brakes, he was going downhill and coming up fast behind a car full of people. He knew he had to go for the ditch but he was able to pick a spot with a huge snow bank."

"What happened?" Clayton asked, his voice reflecting his shock.

"Well, the truck rolled all right, but it could have been worse. Ben walked away without a scratch. We only lost one horse. Two more were cut up quite a bit and we couldn't use them at Edmonton, but they're fine now."

"And you think it wasn't an accident?" Clayton queried.

"It was no accident!" Jenny flared. "The brake line had been cut."

Clayton was silent for a long moment. "Whoever did that wasn't kidding around," he acknowledged. "Someone could have been killed."

"That's right," Josh nodded grimly. "And now the business with the hypodermic needle at Taber and not only that..." he hesitated.

"What?" Clayton demanded.

"Dad thinks there's a chance that Doc Holliday's getting sick might not have been an accident," Josh confided.

"What?" Clayton and Jenny exclaimed in unison.

"I overheard him telling Mom that it's possible to make a horse sick that way by getting him heated up and then giving him too much to drink or letting him eat too much grain," Josh said. "Don't forget, we were away for three days at the rodeo."

"We're going to have to keep our eyes open from now on," Jenny warned.

"But that still doesn't explain the funny business at the rodeos," Clayton reminded them. "Your dad said some of the cowboys have been having some strange bad luck themselves. Even he couldn't figure why anybody would steal Phil Streeter's horse to hurt the D Lazy D."

"Maybe the two aren't related at all," Cindy suggested. "Maybe there are two different mysteries with two different culprits out there."

At that the four teenage travellers lapsed into silence and maneuvered to find comfortable positions in the back seat of the McKannin pickup. In the front seat, Mr. and Mrs. McKannin had listened with interest to the musings of the young passengers, but offered no comment.

It wasn't long before Josh and Jenny had dozed off. As the minutes ticked off, Clayton's gaze wandered from the prairie landscape flashing by outside to the pretty girl sitting at the opposite window. Occasionally, their glances at one another were simultaneous, resulting in an awkward moment which ended each time with Cindy smiling shyly and Clayton clearing his throat. At one point, the throat clearing became so frequent that Mrs. McKannin, with a playful smile, offered Clayton a throat lozenge and expressed the hope that he wasn't allergic to something in the truck. After that, Clayton diligently forced his attention to remain on things outside the pickup and the rest of the trip passed uneventfully.

The Brooks rodeo was a good one for the three contestants in the McKannin cavalcade. During the steer riding, Clayton was perched on the chute above Josh and even helped him with his preparations for his ride. The steer had been all right and the 69 points Josh was awarded by the judges was the third highest of the rodeo to that point with just one day remaining.

Cindy and Jenny had recorded identical 14.8 second times in the barrel racing and were tied for fourth place overall.

As soon as the barrel racing had ended, Clayton received further evidence of the rigorous life of rodeo contestants. Long before the performance was over, the camper was loaded, the horses fed and put back in the horse trailer and the troupe was back on the road. This time the trail headed south. It would involve driving well into the night in order to allow them to make Great Falls before that rodeo's two o'clock start.

To pass some of the time, Clayton leafed through a copy of the program for the Great Falls Rodeo. Mr. McKannin had borrowed one from a cowboy who had already competed there. As he flipped through the list of competitors, Clayton felt a surge of pride as he read the names of his two cousins and Cindy McKannin. Then as he flipped the page one more time, his eye caught the names of the cowboys in the Saddle Bronc Riding. One name seemed to explode off the page and as he saw it, an involuntary shudder went through Clayton's body. The boy couldn't understand why but he had a feeling, a bad feeling, when he saw that name. The name was Lefty Shivers!

Chapter Eleven

The little caravan crossed the border just before midnight. At the border, the only travellers awake were Mrs. McKannin, who was taking a turn at the wheel, and Clayton.

He wouldn't have missed this for the world. One thing Clayton had not done much was travel. His only previous visits to the United States consisted of three brief excursions to Buffalo, New York. His father occasionally got tickets to Sabres hockey games through his business connections and a few times, Clayton got to go along.

But this was different. This was the wild west. Montana was an integral part of the mental picture Clayton had formed of what the west was all about. It was the same picture formed by thousands of urban dwellers whose only contact with the West comes from watching television reruns of old westerns.

But Clayton's eagerness to see Montana and experience it first-hand would have to wait. It was, after all, the middle of the night and pitch black outside. Mrs. McKannin drove only a short way past the border crossing before turning off the road into a campground. At this hour, there were no signs of life in the campground and even the attendant had abandoned his little office for the night. A sign on the door said "Pick a campsite and pay the attendant in the morning."

Mrs. McKannin skillfully maneuvered the truck, camper and horse trailer down a narrow gravel road that led to the campsites. Clayton experienced a faintly eerie sensation as they slowly moved past darkened campers and motorhomes, some with a faint glow coming from the evening's campfire.

"Sure is quiet," he whispered to Mrs. McKannin.

"Sure is," she agreed.

"Sort of gives me the creeps," Clayton confided.

"No need for it to," Mrs. McKannin replied. "It's not much different than a city in the middle of the night. Everybody's sleeping, that's all."

That made Clayton feel a little better. He realized he was more than a little tired himself. The truck's headlights illuminated a vacant spot off to the right and Mrs. McKannin deftly wheeled the truck and trailer into position. A sign indicated this was campsite number sixteen. By then, the others in the truck had begun to wake up, rubbing sleepy eyes and peering into the black night in a futile attempt to get their bearings.

Mrs. McKannin stopped the truck, and shut off the engine. Almost by some pre-arranged plan, a flurry of activity began. Jenny and Cindy stumbled groggily out of the truck and went back to the horse trailer. They unloaded the two horses and tied them to the outside of the trailer for the night.

Mr. and Mrs. McKannin went into the camper and began making up beds for the weary group of travellers. Josh and Clayton busied themselves lowering the hydraulic jacks attached to the outside of the camper. Once in contact with the ground, the four jacks provided added stability for the camper and its occupants.

It wasn't many minutes before the camper in site sixteen was in the same state of quiet and darkness as the others in the sleeping campground. Mr. and Mrs. McKannin and the teenagers exchanged good nights and stillness settled over the crowded but comfortable camper.

Then from his spot next to Josh, Clayton whispered a hushed "Good night, Cindy."

The girl's gentle "Good night, Clayton" came back from across the camper.

However, any thoughts they might have had of a romantically conveyed good night were dashed when Jenny blurted, "Geez, how are ya supposed to get any sleep in here? It sounds like "The Waltons".

"Good night Jen-Boy," Josh chirped cheerfully and everyone burst into laughter. It was a happy way to end what had been a good, but exhausting day.

They rose early the next morning. Breakfast consisted of hastily prepared toast and bacon. Second cups of coffee were taken along as the caravan was once again back on the road headed for Great Falls.

Clayton's silent wish for clear skies was granted and he was soon totally engrossed in the harsh scenery passing outside the window. The country appeared to be more rugged than most of what he had seen in Canada. He was particularly impressed by the flat-topped mountains in the distance. In fact, the scene was right out of a western movie and the more he concentrated, the more he could almost imagine some of the men he'd read about riding over this very ground. Men like Butch Cassidy, the Sundance Kid, the outlaw Tom Horn and even Colonel George Armstrong Custer and his Seventh Cavalry could all have passed over these ridges and through these coulees.

While Clayton lost himself in his dreams of days long past, Josh, Jenny and Cindy passed the time arguing about school, cowboys, cowgirls and rodeos. It was always difficult to get unanimous agreement on any topic when Jenny was part of the discussion. But the three of them did share the exact same opinion on one subject—the Shivers boys. That name brought scowls, clenched fists and nods of agreement whenever it happened to be brought into the conversation.

Eventually the time passed and the skyline of Great Falls came into view, with only an hour to spare before the rodeo. By the time Mr MacKannin had maneuvered the truck and trailer through the bustling center of town to the rodeo grounds, there was just enough time to unload and warm up the barrel-racing horses before the arena had to be cleared for the Grand Entry.

But Great Falls was to prove as unlucky as Brooks had been lucky. It was Cindy's turn to knock down a barrel this time and the penalty took her out of the prize money. Jenny had been having a good run when Sugar stumbled rounding the final barrel. The crowd gasped as for a moment it looked as if horse and rider would take a fall, but the horse recovered its footing and Jenny, who had lost her stirrups and was almost out of the saddle, still brought the horse home in an all-out gallop. The crowd roared its approval for the courage and horsemanship of the Canadian girl, but the stumble slowed their time and Jenny, too, would collect no prize money in Great Falls.

To make matters worse, Josh's steer didn't have much buck in him and Josh had to settle for 58 points, well below the scores of the leaders. Surprisingly, the most disappointed member of the group was Clayton. "What rotten luck!" he fumed. "Here we came all this way and none of us won a dime."

"That's rodeo," Josh replied with a philosophical shrug. "There'll be other days."

The job of packing up after a bad day is much tougher than after a day of winning performances. The travellers doggedly got ready to hit the road one more time for the long drive home.

Suddenly Jenny spoke up. "Mr. McKannin, could we just watch the bronc riding before we go?" she asked.

"Well, I don't know," Mr. McKannin replied. "We really should be..."

"Please," Jenny pleaded. "Just the bronc riding. There's something we just have to see."

"Well, all right," he gave in. "But make sure you're back here the minute its over."

"Right!" Jenny agreed. "Come on," she yelled to the others, "You don't want to miss this."She was off like a shot.

With puzzled looks at one another, Josh, Cindy and Clayton broke into a run in the the direction of the bucking chutes. They were breathless by the time they got to the chutes. The bronc riding was just about to start. "What's the big deal?" Josh grabbed the arm of his sister. "We don't even know who's riding."

"Oh, yes we do," she answered with a grin. Jenny pointed to the far end of the chutes where, in chute number five, the unmistakable figure of Lefty Shivers was getting ready to climb down on the back of a palomino bronc.

"You dragged us over here to watch Lefty Shivers ride?" Clayton asked in disbelief.

"Settle down, Cousin," Jenny said with a wink. "It'll be worth it. Now let's get a little closer." With that she led her dubious followers to a spot where they had a perfect view of Lefty as he prepared to make his ride.

"What's going on?" Clayton demanded in a loud whisper.

"Keep your eyes on that man right there," Jenny answered, pointing to a huge man walking up and down behind the chutes.

He was the biggest cowboy Clayton had ever seen. "Who is he?" he asked her.

"That," she responded, "is Grumpy Kenrod. He's the stock contractor for this rodeo. They don't call him Grumpy for nothing. And you're about to find out why."

"I've got a hunch you're up to something, Jenny Douglas," Josh admonished his sister, though his curiosity made him lean forward for a better look.

The bronc rider in chute number three nodded his head. The gate opened and out he went on a high kicking, showy kind of horse. Moments later, the cowboy in chute four went to work but lasted not much more than half of the required eight seconds.

Now it was Lefty's turn. The announcer told the crowd that the next bronc rider was Canadian Lefty Shivers.

Grumpy Kenrod leaned over the back of the bucking chute to adjust a flank strap, a sheepskin covered leather belt that fits over the horse's flank. As the horse tries to kick off the strap, it has a tendency to buck higher and higher.

Suddenly it happened. The huge contractor let out a roar. "What the Sam..." he blurted and in the same instant reached down and plucked Lefty from the back of the bucking horse with about the same ease that most people pick crumbs off their shirts.

"What did you do to my horse?" he hollered, still holding Lefty about a foot off the ground.

"What...what do you mean?" Lefty's voice wasn't much more than a wheeze.

"His tail! Where's my horse's tail?" Grumpy raged. "You cut my horse's tail off."

"But...but, I thought you wanted me to." Lefty stammered. "That is, they told..."

"I wanted you to?" Grumpy Kenrod's massive frame shook with anger. "You thought I wanted you to cut his tail off? Are you crazy?"

"But they told me you did," Lefty pleaded.

"Told you? Who told you?" the contractor set Lefty down so hard that the smaller man's teeth smashed together with a click that Jenny and the others could plainly hear.

"It was those ki..." Lefty started to say, then clamped his mouth shut, as he realized that his answer would only make things worse.

"Uh...look...I"m sorry, Grumpy," he apologized. "No kiddin', I know it was dumb. I wasn't thinkin'. It won't happen again. Maybe I could pay you or somethin'."

"Pay me or something?" Grumpy's mood was not being helped by the fact that behind the chutes a cascade of laughter was coming from the throng of cowboys and cowgirls who had gathered. Even the announcer was chuckling as he referred to "a slight commotion that will delay our next ride for a moment."

"You're not gettin' on my horse," Grumpy leaned closer to Lefty's frightened face. "Do you hear me? I'm not letting that palomino out into the arena with most of his tail missing so you can forget it."

"But I paid fifty bucks entry fees," Lefty sputtered.

"Well, then I guess we'll call it square," Grumpy growled at him, "because I figure that horse's tail is worth exactly fifty dollars. And one more thing, Shivers," he shook his finger in front of Lefty's nose. "If you ever touch a single hair on one of my animals again, I'm going to find out what you look like without any hair. Do you understand?"

"Yes, sir, Mister Grumpy...uh...Kenrod... I mean, I ..... understand, Grumpy."

With that, the hostile stock contractor stomped off toward chute number six. Slowly Lefty's fear began to be replaced first by humiliation at the laughter that was ringing in his ears and then by anger when he realized he'd been had. He began looking around. It was obvious he was looking for someone.

"Maybe we ought to get out of here," Clayton suggested.

"Nothing to worry about," Jenny replied, nonchalantly. `It's not us he's looking for." And with a knowing toss of her head, she started off in the direction of the camper.

Quickly the other three caught up to her.

"I know you're behind this thing, but I don't know how," Josh stated.

"Oh, it was nothing, really," Jenny sniffed.

"Come on," Clayton coaxed. "Let us in on it."

"Yeah, fess up, Jenny," Cindy chimed in.

"Well, okay," Jenny dropped her voice to a confidential level. "Actually the idea just popped into my head when I saw that creep Lefty Shivers standing at the concession stand. He had that typical arrogant look on his face. Well, I knew he wouldn't listen to me," she went on. "But Miles has been sweet on me for a long time so I figured I'd just play him up a little."

"When did all this take place?" Josh asked her.

"During the Grand Entry and the Steer Riding," came the reply. "I guess I missed your ride today."

"Doesn't matter," Josh replied. "It wasn't much anyway."

"So tell us what happened," Clayton urged.

"Well, I cozied up to Miles like crazy, telling him how great I thought him and his brother are," Jenny continued. "And the stupid jerk fell for the whole thing. And that's when I told him that I'd heard some of the cowboys talking with Grumpy and how Grumpy had said that this horse would only buck if his tail was cut short. Just up to the bone, I told him, so as not to hurt it."

By now tears of laughter were welling up in Jenny's eyes. She could hardly tell the rest of her story. "Well, the next thing I saw," she finally continued, "Miles was telling Clint Runner what I'd said and the two of them went skedaddling off to clue good old Lefty in on how to win the rodeo."

"I can't believe anybody would be that stupid," Clayton sputtered between fits of laughter.

"Nobody but the Shivers boys," Cindy too was laughing uncontrollably.

Josh, always the more serious one, shook his head doggedly. "You know what I'm afraid of? When Lefty finds out who was behind this, he'll be out for revenge. That could spell even more trouble for the D Lazy D."

Jenny was quick to disagree. "I doubt it," she replied confidently. "Do you really think Miles is going to admit to his big brother that he was hoodwinked by a girl? And a Douglas to boot? I think Miles will do just about anything to keep good ol' Lefty from finding out the truth," she concluded.

"You know," Josh answered slowly, "you just may be right at that." A grin began to spread over his face. "Sister of mine, you are some sneaky lady and I'm awful glad you're on our side."

It was a jovial group that arrived back at the McKannin camper ready to set out for home. Somehow the long drive didn't look nearly as bad any more. Great Falls had proved to be quite a memorable rodeo after all.

Still, Clayton rode part of the way in thoughtful silence. Though he preferred not to talk about it, he still had eerie feelings about Miles and Lefty Shivers. Miles was sure to be totally embarrassed at being fooled by Jenny. And if Lefty ever found out the truth about the prank, he would surely want revenge. Clayton silently reminded himself that it would be wise to be extra alert from now on whenever Lefty or Miles was around. He was sure Josh was right. They hadn't heard the end of the Shivers boys.

Chapter Twelve

Spring drifted gently into summer bringing with it lush, rolling fields of grain and a neverending green blanket of trees in full leaf that stretched westward to the Rockies. With summer came warm evenings with soft breezes blowing down from the mountains. Like unmoving sentinels standing guard over some unseen fortress, the mountains were just visible in the hazy distance.

For Clayton, it was a time of learning more about his new way of life and about himself. It was inevitable that he would become the object of much teasing from both of his cousins and his uncle. Aunt Laura was more understanding and sympathetic. She said nothing and merely smiled knowingly when the subject of Cindy came up at the dinner table, as it often did. Then came the end of the school year which brought sighs of relief, shouts of joy and the sight of notebooks and pencils being tossed skyward. More importantly though, the summer holidays meant more time for riding. After a few weeks of hard work, Clayton was well on his way to becoming a very capable rider.

Josh and Jenny had picked out an old buckskin mare for Clayton to learn on. They had both learned to ride on the same horse when they were younger. At eighteen years old, she was the oldest and one of the quietest horses on the ranch but still showed a good burst of speed when it was needed to keep up with Josh's chestnut, Scooter, or Jenny's ranch horse, a tall gelding called Chief.

Clayton spent a couple of hours in the saddle every day as he, Josh and Jenny probed every square inch of the Douglas property from the stand of tall poplars that formed the northern border of the D Lazy D, to the highway east of the ranch, and all the way to where the land sloped sharply away to a clear stream running along the ranch's south and west boundaries.

In the meantime, the work had begun in earnest with Doc Holliday. Clayton spent a good part of each day brushing and grooming the stallion, letting the horse become more and more accustomed to human contact. It would be some time before any actual riding would take place.

Under Jenny's watchful eye, Clayton went through a daily process of first sacking the horse out, then putting a blanket and saddle on him and walking him around the corral. The sacking out consisted of rubbing Doc Holliday all over with a blanket to quiet him down. As the horse became accustomed and less agitated by the contact, Clayton lightly flapped the blanket against the animal's back, sides and legs. The idea was to simulate any kind of contact the horse might undergo when being ridden and get him used to it.

When the sacking out was completed, the saddle blanket was placed on the horse's back. Then came the saddle, which was gently cinched, just enough to keep it in place. It was left on him, sometimes for an hour at a time. Gradually Doc seemed to get getting over his initial fear and dislike of the saddle.

He still occasionally crow-hopped around the corral, and once in a while reared to show his displeasure. Jenny told Clayton that it would be a long, slow process but both agreed that it was worth the time and effort.

Weekends, of course, were rodeo times and Clayton found himself looking forward to the now familiar routine. Thursday was spent getting the equipment, vehicles and stock ready for transport. Friday saw the entire Douglas outfit heading down the highway to places the boy from the east had usually never heard of. Red Deer, Hand Hills, Lethbridge and Williams Lake—all took on special meaning to Clayton and, like every cowboy and cowgirl, he came to feel at home in their rodeo arenas.

But one name meant a little more than all the others. Its approach heralded an annual time of feverish activity on the Douglas spread, activity that was being duplicated in one form or another all over southern Alberta and beyond.

The Calgary Stampede was just a few days away. Every spare minute was being put to use in repairing and cleaning equipment, sprucing up the vehicles and shining boots, cleaning and ironing clothes and even, at least for the men, getting haircuts. Clayton was beginning to wonder if any single rodeo could be worth all this fuss, but he was assured by all of the members of the Douglas family that it most certainly was.

"This isn't just a rodeo," Aunt Laura explained over dinner one evening. " It's like the Stanley Cup, the World Series, the Miss Canada Pageant, a Garth Brooks concert and a federal election campaign all rolled into one."

"That's right, Clayton," Uncle Roy added, "In Calgary you'll see the best cowboys in the world competing. The rodeo is ten days long, and the finals are on the last day. That's when the top hands from the first nine days compete for fifty thousand dollars in each event and that's just for one day."

"It's not just the prize money either," Josh chimed in. "There's a whole lot of prestige that goes along with winning at the Calgary Stampede."

"Not only that, but all the cutest cowboys are there," Jenny enthused. "It's great."

Unlike the other rodeos Clayton had attended, where one stock contractor came in with all the stock for that rodeo, for the Calgary Stampede a number of stock contractors were invited to bring only their best horses and bulls. This ensured that the cowboys would be competing on the best stock available. A sort of friendly competition existed among the stock contractors as each hoped his animals would outperform the stock of the others.

This year's Stampede had extra meaning and excitement for the Douglas family. Josh had realized his goal and was entered in the Boys' Steer Riding. He would be riding on the third day. Unfortunately, Jenny had not won enough money to meet the eligibility rule for the Stampede Barrel Racing competition. She unselfishly made the transition from competitor to observer by becoming her brother's number one fan.

At first glance, as the family made final preparations for the short journey into Calgary, the excitement was so great that it was difficult to tell who was actually riding. As the great event approached, Clayton was as nervous as everyone else.

Thursday finally came and it was time to head for the Stampede City. The Stampede was to start the next day with a morning parade kicking off ten days of non-stop activity. The furthest thing from everyone's mind as they made the trip to the city from the D Lazy D was the series of mysterious happenings that had been plaguing the rodeo circuit. Since the theft of Phil Streeter's horse during the Taber rodeo, no further incidents had taken place. Almost everyone had concluded that the culprit was probably someone not directly involved with rodeo who had probably moved on. As for the D Lazy D, no further mysterious mishaps had taken place there either and everyone had begun to relax their guard a little.

The first morning of the Stampede, Clayton was excused from his duties and allowed to play tourist. He and Aunt Laura took in the parade while Roy, Jenny, Josh and the ever-present Ben Bradley took care of getting the stock looked after.

The first Calgary Stampede had taken place in 1912. Since then it had grown to the point that people actually came from all over the world to witness the spectacle. Clayton was amazed to see the city's streets lined several people deep to catch a glimpse of the parade as it passed by. He had often witnessed Toronto's famous Santa Claus parade, but here there was a difference. Almost everywhere he looked, people were dressed like cowboys. Two elderly ladies passed in front of him. They were chatting and laughing like school girls. Each of the ladies had the traditional white stetson perched on her head. As Aunt Laura and Clayton looked for a spot to watch the parade from, he glanced down a side street. There, in a roped-off area, a band was pounding out a tune and a square-dance caller was calling out instructions. The dancers looked like they had never square-danced before but all of them, Clayton figured there must be forty or fifty people, were having a terrific time.

Clayton couldn't help himself. He was quickly caught up in the enthusiasm. At last he and Aunt

Laura wriggled their way into a spot between a television cruiser and temporary set of bleachers. From here they would be able to see perfectly. It wasn't long before the first section of the parade came into view. A huge pipe and bugle band led the way. The musicians were playing a jaunty tune and as the band came closer, Clayton was able to make out from the banner held by two of the majorettes that the band was from a high school in Toronto! Clayton doffed his hat and waved. He cheered so hard he was in danger of losing his voice the first morning of the Stampede. Aunt Laura joined in to welcome and show her appreciation for the visitors from the East.

As the parade went on, she provided a running commentary for Clayton and proved to be a source of great knowledge. Clayton learned that Indians had always been a major focal point of the Stampede. He marveled at the majesty of the various tribes wearing the brilliant costumes of their heritage as they rode slowly down the streets on brightly painted horses. He learned too, about a number of breeds of horses from the showy Arabians to the high-stepping American Saddlebreds, all of which were represented in the parade. And there were the usual floats, bands and clowns which form a necessary part of every parade. But most of all, the Calgary Stampede parade was cowboys, Indians and horses. And Clayton couldn't for a second take his eyes off the panorama of western culture that was passing in front of him.

Then it was over and it was time for Clayton and Aunt Laura to make their way, on foot for there was no other way to travel on parade morning, back to the Stampede grounds. They would be just in time for the start of the rodeo.

Clayton was almost overwhelmed. He had never seen anything like the color and spirit of the whole city as it embarked on what Calgarians called "Stampede Week." Having visited the Canadian National Exhibition in Toronto, he wasn't especially awed by the myriad of activities, lights and noise that filled almost every inch of Stampede Park.

But when he arrived at the Stampede's rodeo arena, it was quite another matter. Everywhere he looked he saw pomp and pageantry, and a few hundred feet away from the arena a magnificent grandstand was jammed with thousands of spectators. A constant buzz of pre-rodeo excitement rose from the grandstand.

The Douglas rodeo string had had eight bulls, five bareback horses and six saddle broncs selected for the Stampede, but that first afternoon only three horses and three bulls were in the draw so the workload had been light for the working members of the family. One of the bulls that was to be in the afternoon performance was Little Bighorn, the unpleasant rogue that had given Roy and Clayton a bad time that long ago day in the corral. Clayton was eager to see the bull in action in the rodeo arena.

There was more tension than usual behind the chutes. Cowboys paced up and down. The joking and kibbitzing that normally filled the minutes before the start of a rodeo were almost totally absent.

From the announcer's stand, the voice of Hank Parker seemed to carry even more excitement that it usually did. Even the stock seemed nervous, as if the animals too could sense the importance of the event. There was more than the usual amount of snorting, pawing and head tossing as they were loaded into the chutes.

Soon it was underway. As always, the Grand Entry preceded the rodeo, but never had Clayton seen a Grand Entry to match this. Flags representing every province in Canada, the United States, the Canadian Professional Rodeo Association and each of the stock contractors were carried into the arena by mounted riders colorfully garbed in red and gold matched western outfits.

Then as the Stampede Band played and marched through the arena, the mounted color party wove its way intricately in and out of the rows of the band in an effect that was nothing short of spectacular. Suddenly the music crescendoed and stopped. Almost as if touched by a wand, every member of the Grand Entry cast, both mounted and on foot, came to a perfectly choreographed halt that faced the grandstand.

With the tension by this time at practically a fever pitch, Clayton saw cowboys' jaws tightening and loosening as they tried to control their own mounting excitement. Then it was time for the playing of "Oh Canada" and thousands of cowboy hats were removed in unison at the chutes and in the stands as the final moments before the start of the rodeo ticked away.

The spectacular Grand Entry ended and the rodeo began. Clayton watched spellbound as with each ride and each run the crowd roared its approval. It seemed that the cheering was just as loud when there was a bone-rattling spill as when a cowboy turned in a great ride or fast time.

The afternoon seemed to pass in the wink of an eye, and the first day of rodeo was drawing to a conclusion. The Calf Roping was the last event before the Bull Riding. Clayton was jotting the times of the ropers in his program. The last roper was a man named Jame Gartens, a better-than-average calf roper and bronc rider from Kamloops, British Columbia. Clayton had seen him rope calves and ride saddle broncs before and knew he was good. Hank Parker was telling the crowd that Jame Gartens was tied for third in the Canadian All-Round standings. The cowboy Gartens was tied with was Len Tucker, the genial character who had befriended Clayton and Josh during their fistfight with Miles Shivers and Clint Runner. Lefty Shivers was in the lead for the All-Round and Phil Streeter who, in spite of having had his best roping horse stolen, was in second place.

Clayton leaned forward from the walkway behind the bucking chutes to get a better look at Jame Gartens, who looked to be about ready. The cowboy nodded his head and the calf was released. Instantly, Gartens, mounted on a powerful bay horse, was in pursuit. His arm circled his head once, then twice, and the rope snaked its way toward its destination around the calf's neck. As if it had eyes, the rope found its mark. Simultaneously the roper's well-trained horse was braking hard to a halt and Gartens was dismounting on the run. Clayton knew that this was the part of the event that the cowboy excelled at.

There probably wasn't a roper in Canada quicker at coming off his horse, getting down the rope to the calf, putting the animal on the ground and making the tie. This time, however, the unexpected happened. The calf was brought to a momentary stop by the rope, then continued on its way.

The rope had snapped!

At first, Clayton couldn't believe what he had

seen. He had never witnessed such a thing before. It was obviously a surprise for Jame Gartens too. He had already been off the horse and part way toward the calf when the rope broke. The cowboy picked up the broken end of the rope and looked at it in total disbelief. He tossed it away in disgust as announcer Hank Parker asked for and got a sympathetic round of applause from the crowd for the unlucky roper. It was a particularly bad blow for Jame Gartens as a no-time at the Calgary Stampede would certainly diminish his chances of winning the All-Round Championship.

Then it was time for Bull Riding, the last event on the program. Clayton and Josh both tensed up. They were hoping the D Lazy D bulls, especially Little Bighorn, would put on a good show. Clayton asked his cousin who had drawn Little Bighorn. "It's Cullen Rawlinson from Comanche, Oklahoma," Josh told him. "He's a good rider and he might be able to go the eight seconds on him, but the problem with this bull is what happens after the ride. He'll go after anything he sees including cowboys and clowns, but then I guess you know all about that."

"Yeah, I sure do," Clayton nodded his head ruefully. "Tub Willoughby better be on his toes," he added.

Tub Willoughby was working with a second clown named Doolie Kent. Tub was jumping up and down in his gaudy clown barrel while Doolie Kent stood nearby ready to go to the aid of a cowboy in trouble.

The boys pressed closer as the time for Rawlinson's ride on Little Bighorn came closer. "This is it," Josh said, pointing to chute number four.

A wiry cowboy with a long, dark mustache and black stetson was taking his final wrap with his bull rope. Cullen Rawlinson then slid forward on the bull's back so that he was almost sitting on his right hand, now tightly bound into the rope. He lifted his left arm above his head and nodded, signalling for the gate to be opened.

As Josh had said, Little Bighorn wasn't the stylish bucking bull that Bad Medicine was, but it was his ornery meanness that made him both hard to ride and hard to get away from afterwards.

The Oklahoma cowboy was as good as Josh had predicted. Although Little Bighorn twisted, gyrated and generally tried to make things unpleasant for the man on his back, Cullen Rawlinson was still aboard when the horn signaled the eight second limit. Since pickup men aren't used in Bull Riding, it is up to the cowboy to get off on his own, with assistance from the clowns who try to distract the bull.

Rawlinson, with the crowd wildly cheering his successful ride, got off safely and scrambled back to the chutes as Doolie Kent, just inches from Little Bighorn's massive head, got his attention. Then the clown circled the bull, twice slapping his nose, and led him to the barrel from which Tub Willoughby protruded with his "dukes up" like a boxer ready to do battle. At the last second, the comical clown disappeared inside the barrel. Little Bighorn hit it with all the force of his fifteen hundred pounds and the painted barrel went rolling and tumbling down the arena with Tub inside. For a full minute the entertainment continued as Doolie Kent rolled the barrel toward the bull who angrily butted it back. Every once in a while the crowd would see Tub's head pop out of the barrel and blow a kiss in the direction of the infuriated animal, then disappear inside again as Little Bighorn charged.

Then Josh and Clayton and thousands of spectators watched as Doolie Kent backed away from the protection of the barrel, at first a little ways, then a little more, then still more. Little Bighorn was also backing up in the opposite direction from the barrel, watching, waiting and pawing the ground angrily.

Suddenly Doolie began running at the barrel at full speed. The bull hesitated, then it too charged the barrel from the opposite direction. The two arrived at almost the same moment. Doolie Kent got there just a split second ahead of Little Bighorn, and the clown jumped, hit the barrel with one foot and leaped up and over the charging animal which threw its head up in an attempt to hit the object now sailing over him.

The rodeo clown landed behind the bull and waved his hat to the crowd which had been collectively holding its breath and now erupted with a roar of approval. Little Bighorn shook his massive shoulders and almost as if he realized there would be another day, trotted haughtily out of the arena through the open gate. The first performance of the Calgary Stampede was over, and what a performance it had been!

Roy approached the two boys, his face wreathed in a smile. "Well, the D Lazy D stock put on a pretty good show, don't you think? Particularly our grouchy friend over there." He jerked a thumb in the direction of Little Bighorn who was now in a pen behind the arena.

"You're not kidding, Dad," Josh agreed, "The whole rodeo was great."

"Yeah, but it's too bad Jame Garten's rope broke," Clayton interjected, "He would have had a really fast time on that calf. That was really tough luck."

"Tough luck had nothing to do with it," his uncle responded, his face becoming serious. "That rope was cut, boys. Whoever our rodeo marauder is, it looks like he's struck again!"

Chapter Thirteen

The next nine days were easily the most memorable of Clayton Findlay's life. There were so many highlights, he would have trouble recalling them all afterwards. The second night of the Stampede, he joined the whole Douglas family at the world-famous chuckwagon races. Ben Bradley and his wife Rose, a plump, friendly woman with red cheeks that looked like they had just been pinched, also went along. And, happily for Clayton, the McKannins, who had come into town for the rodeo that afternoon, rounded out the group.

This time they were actually in the mammoth grandstand watching the action unfold before them. Clayton went to considerable trouble to ensure that he was seated next to Cindy McKannin. The task was made doubly difficult by the antics of Jenny who, with an impish gleam in her eye, was doing all she could to thwart the two starry-eyed teenagers.

What took place on the track in front of them took Clayton's breath away. He was hard-pressed to decide whether the excitement and danger of what the announcer called the "Rangeland Derby" was even greater than that of the Bull Riding.

As was the custom throughout the grandstand during the chuckwagon races, friendly bets were made everywhere. Clayton and Cindy teamed up to win most of the twenty-five cent bets and between them ended the evening about three dollars ahead. This modest windfall would give them a start on the midway rides when the chuckwagon races and evening stage show were concluded.

The roar and dust of the wagon races had barely

died away when a huge stage was chugged into place by an equally huge caterpillar tractor. The stage show itself was a blaze of color and music, quite unlike anything Clayton had ever seen. Capping it off was a dazzling aerial display of fireworks with each new burst of splendor apparently trying to out-do the previous one. It was a night he would not soon forget and it wasn't over yet.

Midways were not new to Clayton. What was new was seeing and experiencing it in the company of Cindy McKannin. Clayton especially enjoyed the roller coaster where the force of the rapidly hurtling coaster threw Cindy against him. He liked the smell of her hair and the feel of it as it blew softly against his face. But even "nights-of-a-lifetime" have to come to an end. The three families yelled goodnight to one another over the roar of the wildly spinning Enterprise thrill-ride and the screams of its deliciously frightened riders.

No sooner were the Douglases and Clayton out of earshot of the others than Jenny could contain herself no more. "Dad," she began loudly, "is there anything worse than two people looking moon-faced at each other all night long? I mean, surely you and Mom didn't look like that." She finished her harangue with a gesture in the general direction of Clayton.

"Oh now, Jenny Douglas," Clayton rebuked her. "It's no different than the way you behaved in Great Falls with your sweetie, Miles Shivers." At that the quick-tongued, red-haired girl was forced to clamp her lips tightly together. She couldn't respond to the tease without letting her parents know about the prank she had pulled on Lefty and Miles in Great Falls. Everyone had agreed that was one secret it might be best not to share with adults—at least for the time being.

The next morning was an early one. The stock had to be watered, then sorted for the day's rodeo. Flank straps, halters, spurs and boots were given fresh coats of spit and polish.

Len Tucker, who was scheduled to compete that day, sauntered by and stopped for a minute to chat before moving on. When the work was done, Roy announced that the whole family were to be his guests for breakfast at the Big Four Building. The Big Four was one of the world's largest ice curling rinks which had been transformed into an exhibit center for the Stampede. Over breakfast, Roy told them the special meal together was to celebrate the realization of Josh's dream. That dream — riding at the Calgary Stampede — would be fulfilled that afternoon.

When the moment finally came, Josh was calm and ready. He was first out in the Boys' Steer Riding and drew a good steer. His 77 point ride tied him for the lead to that point. Josh looked like a good bet for the finals, which were still a week away.

Everyone was hoping that the series of disasters which had befallen so many of the cowboys wouldn't strike Len Tucker as he prepared to make his run in the Calf Roping. Fortunately, all went smoothly for the veteran hand as he turned in a rapid 10.2 seconds. Like Josh, he had taken a big step on the way to the finals. Later, Len rode his bull the required eight seconds, but marked only 64 points on the animal. That score was not likely to help him make the finals in Bull Riding. Still, the easy-going cowboy was beaming afterwards as he received congratulations for his effort in the Roping.

And so it went, day after day, as new thrills replaced old ones. It was a time that Clayton wanted never to end. But inevitably, the end did come. First, however, there were the all-important Finals on the last afternoon of the Stampede. Two days before, a torrential downpour had turned the arena into a muddy swamp making the footing difficult for everyone — cowboys, stock and clowns included. The day before the Finals had been overcast and threatening more rain. But to everyone's relief, it never came.

The Sunday morning of the Finals dawned clear with blue skies and not a cloud to be seen. By rodeo time that afternoon, the sun had combined with the efforts of the Stampede grounds crew to dry out the arena and conditions were nearly perfect.

The tension was even greater than it had been on that first day of the Calgary Stampede. More money and glory would be won that afternoon than at any other rodeo anywhere, and there wasn't a cowboy or spectator who didn't feel a surge of anticipation through his or her veins.

The Calgary Stampede attracts a large contingent of American cowboys, many of whom rodeo year round and are outstanding competitors. So it wasn't surprising when the first two events, Bareback Riding and Steer Wrestling, were won by contestants from south of the line. Lefty Shivers, who had also made it to the finals in Bull Riding, ended up second among the Steer Wrestlers.

Then it was time for the Boys' Steer Riding. All of the steer riders had competed on two different animals to qualify for the finals. Josh had finished tied for second. His 152 points had been equalled by Clint Runner and topped by only one cowboy— Miles Shivers with 153.

"Well, at least he won't be able to say the draw was rigged this time," Clayton thought to himself as he watched the first steer riders make their rides. Josh would ride right after Clint Runner. Miles Shivers would be last out. The scores the boys recorded in the Finals would be added to their previous marks and the cowboy with the highest total would be the winner.

Clint Runner looked determined as he settled down on his steer in chute number two. Several cowboys assisted the youngster as he made his final preparations. Then, with teeth gritted, he nodded his head and the gate opened. In spite of their fight, Clayton found himself pulling for Runner to make the klaxon. And he did. It was an excellent ride. The judges awarded the boy with 78 points for a 230 point total on his three steers. It meant that Josh would need a super ride to beat him.

Chute three was a hive of activity as Roy and Ben helped Josh get ready. Clayton leaned over the chute and said quietly to his cousin, "79 points will do it. Should be a snap. I'm counting on you." Josh looked up and flashed a quick grin at Clayton. Then he slid forward on his steer and nodded his head. The steer was bigger than most that day and when the gate opened, it exploded out of the chute with a furious unleashing of power and speed.

Josh's steer spun left for a couple of jumps, then came out of it with a high jarring leap, crashing down hard on his front feet, back legs high in the air, his back at almost a ninety degree angle to the ground. Then the steer came around hard to the right, jumping and kicking out at the same time. All the while, Josh stuck like glue and furiously jabbed his heels into the animal's sides, in an effort to aid his balance and impress the judges who look for the rider's ability to use his feet. The klaxon sounded and the ride ended with a roar of approval from the crowd.

Then came the wait for the score. A suspenseful silence settled over the arena. Then the familiar voice of Hank Parker pierced the air with the words "Eighty-one points for Josh Douglas! That gives him a total of 233 on three steers and moves him into the lead."

That left only Miles Shivers for the final ride. He would be coming out of chute number one. His brother Lefty and two other burly cowboys were assisting the boy. The gate opened and Clayton could see at once that Shivers had drawn a tough steer, the kind that's hard to ride but can make a winner of any cowboy able to last the eight seconds. The steer went straight out for the first three jumps, then started a turn to the right. Suddenly the animal dived back left. It was a move which surprised Miles, who was thrust over to one side. Desperately the young cowboy strained to get back into good position on the steer. The animal jerked hard to the left one more time. The move put its rider virtually upside down in mid-air for an instant before catapulting him hard to the ground just a split second before the horn. The crowd groaned partly from disappointment and partly out of concern as it looked like the kind of fall that could leave a cowboy injured. One thing Miles Shivers wasn't, however, was soft. He got up, slamming his right fist into his left palm and kicking his crumpled stetson across the arena. Tub Willoughby mimicked the angry youngster and sent his outlandish red and white striped cowboy hat across the arena as the crowd's concern turned to glee.

Meanwhile, Clayton was shaking his cousin's hand so hard Josh's arm was in danger of coming out of its socket. He had won! Josh Douglas was the Boys' Steer Riding Champion at the Calgary Stampede. Both boys beamed their pride.

Clint Runner, who had wound up second, sauntered over and offered a hand in congratulations. "Nice goin' Josh," he said sincerely.

"Thanks, Clint, you made a real good ride yourself," Josh replied.

"Thanks," the Indian boy replied. "By the way, that was a pretty good trick your sister pulled on us down at Great Falls." It was obvious from the grin on Clint's angular face that he was not displeased with what had happened.

"Glad to hear you're not mad about it," Josh grinned.

"Heck, no, not me," Clint replied with a chuckle. "Although I sure can't say the same for Lefty and Miles. Me, I figure being fooled by that sister of yours is no shame anyway."

"Yeah, and being second at the Calgary Stampede is nothing to be ashamed of either," Clayton noted.

"Thanks," Clint Runner answered. "Say, what did you say your name was?"

"Clayton, Clayton Findlay."

"You got a middle name?" asked Clint.

"James," was the reply. "Why?"

"Seems to me we ought to call you C. J. or something like that. Clayton isn't a real western handle," Clint Runner suggested.

For a reason he couldn't explain, Clayton felt his old resentment for the west rise within him. The feeling died quickly but he replied just the same, "Thanks, but I think I'll stick to Clayton."

The discussion ended and attention was directed to the Calf Roping chute where the Final in that event was already underway.

In the major events the scores were not cumulative. The top ten cowboys over the first nine days of competition were meeting in sudden-death action. Each would compete once, then the top four from that group would compete a second time. The best total score from among those four contestants would determine the champion, who would win the whopping fifty thousand dollars.

The calf ropers completed their first runs. Len Tucker came out with the second fastest time of 9.9 seconds. Now the four fastest ropers would make their second run. For a while it looked as if good fortune was finally with the likable cowboy. He was the second last man to rope in the group of four and he was lightning fast, adding a 9.7 seconds to his earlier 9.9 for a 19.6 total for his two runs.

The last man out was a Californian named Jud Parradine, who had been World Champion in the event on two separate occasions. Parradine wasn't to be denied. Clayton had never seen anybody that fast. Once the calf was on the ground, the man's hands were a blur as he wrapped three of the struggling animal's legs in the customary two loops and half-hitch knot.

Even before Hank Parker gave the time over the public address system, both Clayton and Josh knew that Len Tucker, the perennial hardluck cowboy, would have to settle for second again. The announcer confirmed that fact when he gave the time for Parradine as an incredible 8.8 seconds. Together with his 9.8 on the first run, it gave him a total of 18.6, a full second faster than Len.

And so the Calgary Stampede ended. It had been an experience which neither Josh, the champion, nor Clayton, the first-time visitor, would ever forget. The Douglas rodeo stock had performed very well, so Roy Douglas and Ben Bradley were happy too. Aunt Laura and Rose Bradley had enjoyed ten days away from the hectic pace of ranch life. And Jenny, well, she had a knack for having a good time wherever she was and whatever she was doing.

Yet, as the happy caravan made its way back home, Clayton was thoughtful and quiet. He was riding next to Josh and Ben in the stock liner. There was something he couldn't get out of his mind. As they were leaving the Stampede grounds, they had met up with Len Tucker. Ben Bradley had rolled down the window and yelled, "Great job, Len, congratulations."

Len had grinned and called back, "Thanks, I'll take a second at the Calgary Stampede anytime I can get it. It's a whole lot better than a lot of other folks did." And the big man waved and headed off toward his own camper.

What was bothering Clayton was something he had seen in Len Tucker's expression, or at least, thought he had seen. Though the familiar grin never left the cowboy's face, Clayton thought he had seen a flicker of an emotion, an emotion he didn't think Len possessed. That fleeting look had lasted only a second, but spoke of something more than pride — of envy, of a man tired of always being second, a man desperately wanting to win just once.

Chapter Fourteen

The day had finally come — the day Clayton and Jenny had been anticipating for a long time. Today they would find out if the long hours of hard work and patience had paid off. Today Clayton would ride Doc Holliday, or, at least, try to ride him. Roy's words rang in their ears as they assembled as nonchalantly as possible for breakfast. "The first time you get thrown off — end of experiment." Both knew that this day would either be one of the best of their lives or one of the worst.

There was a Saturday morning custom in the Douglas household that on those weekends when the family wasn't at a rodeo, the men cooked the meals. So, Roy and Josh were busily preparing scrambled eggs, hash brown potatoes and fried ham. Clayton was setting the table.

Hard as they tried to hide it, everyone was feeling more tense than usual. The usually placid Laura Douglas sat at the table thoughtfully sipping her coffee, and staring long and hard into her cup. Next to her, Jenny was a bundle of nerves. Her normal stream of morning conversation was noticeably absent as she concentrated on the fork she was spinning around on the table cloth. Clayton was polite, almost formal, as he poured juice for Jenny and his Aunt Laura. At the stove, Josh and his dad worked in silence. At the back door, even Casey seemed to sense that this was no ordinary day. He listlessly stood up, laid down and changed positions repeatedly in a futile effort to find a spot he liked.

When the breakfast was served, the usual scramble for the platters didn't occur. Instead, each member of the family took a bare minimum of the breakfast fare. No one was able to do more than pick unenthusiastically at what was in front of him. Even Josh, whose appetite was the source of much good-natured kidding, wasn't in the mood to do justice to what was ordinarily his favorite meal.

The breakfast finally dispensed with, Roy, Josh and Clayton washed and put away the dishes. Jenny stood vacantly staring out the kitchen window, while Laura halfheartedly applied a few stitches to an embroidery project she was working on. What conversation there was, was brief, consisting mostly of one syllable utterances. Each family member seemed lost in his or her own thoughts about what lay ahead.

It wasn't that they weren't confident. Jenny, particularly, knew that the preparations for this moment had been thorough and painstaking. She would have bet a year's allowance that any horse that had been brought along this slowly and carefully would behave for a rider. But Doc Holliday wasn't any horse. He was a bronc, as wild a bronc as had ever lived. What if there was something inside him that just wouldn't let him be tamed? What if a horse his age just couldn't change? What if …?

Clayton wasn't afraid, but he was certainly nervous. He knew how much was at stake but he also realized that both he and Doc Holliday had come a long way under Jenny's persistent tutelage.

Josh and Jenny headed out the door to do chores while Clayton helped his uncle finish up in the kitchen. Clayton tried to tell himself that by lunch time, just a few hours away, it would all be over and everything would have gone perfectly. Try as he might to relax, his mouth formed a thin line of concentration on his youthful face. No matter how

112

hard he tried to dispel any negative thoughts from his mind, there persisted that one nagging little shred of doubt. Like Jenny, he couldn't be absolutely certain that what had once been the wildest horse on the rodeo circuit was now tamed.

The kitchen back in order, it was time to head for the corral. On the way Clayton, accompanied by his aunt and uncle, met up with Josh and Jenny returning from feeding the bulls, the last on their list of chores. Together they walked to Doc Holliday's corral. Clayton's nervousness was building. He hadn't even been this apprehensive during the last week of school in June when he had been writing his final tests for the year.

Before breakfast, Clayton had draped the saddle, blanket and bridle over the top rail of the corral fence. He had wanted to give the stallion every opportunity to feel comfortable with the equipment.

As the group approached the corral, Doc Holliday was calmly nibbling at one of the stirrups. He certainly looked relaxed.

While Roy, Laura and Josh took up positions atop the corral fence to watch the goings on, Jenny and Clayton quietly and quickly saddled the big black horse. They went through the steps carefully but without undo concern, hoping not to alert the horse to any of their own nervousness. If that were to happen, Doc Holliday might become excited and act more unpredictably.

Clayton, who by now had spent dozens of hours on horseback at the D Lazy D, tried to tell himself that this was just another ride, no more and no less important or difficult than any other. But while his brain was trying to give the rest of his body that message, there were parts of him that apparently had some doubt. He was especially aware of his legs, which seemed to Clayton to have about as much strength as a bowl of Aunt Laura's Jello Surprise.

At last the saddle blanket and saddle were in place, the cinch had been tightened and the bridle was on and adjusted to ensure that Doc Holliday felt no discomfort. At that point, Jenny finally spoke.

"All right Cousin, you know what to do. We've done hours of ground work with Doc so he knows his turns and what 'whoa' means. He should be fine if you don't get going too fast. I'd walk him for a while first. Then when you get on, remember what I told you. Feel like you are a part of the horse and he is part of you."

"Right," Clayton replied with a terse nod. For three or four minutes he circled the corral with Doc Holliday. It was a small corral with a high fence, specially designed for breaking and training colts.

After a couple of circuits around the enclosure, Clayton led the horse to the center of the corral. He brought the reins over the stallion's head and placed his left foot in the left stirrup of the saddle. He spoke quietly to the horse. "Okay, now fella. Easy now. Nothing to it, easy now." Then in one smooth motion he swung up and into the saddle.

Clayton was careful not to put any pressure against the horse's sides with his legs. He wouldn't do that until he actually wanted the powerful stallion to move. For a while he just sat astride the horse watching him and letting him get the feel of a rider on his back. Doc Holliday's ears were pricked up and slightly ahead and Clayton knew that meant the horse was alert and attentive.

"So far, so good," Clayton said softly. "Atta boy. Easy now. Nothing to worry about. Good boy." Then with a barely audible cluck of his tongue, Clayton gently tapped the horse's rump with a riding crop to ask him to walk. At the same time, he applied slight pressure with his legs in order for the stallion to start getting accustomed to leg cues. For a second, Doc Holliday seemed a little confused and pranced to the side.

"Easy, boy, whoa, now, whoa, Doc," Clayton spoke to the stallion. When the horse had stopped, Clayton tried once more. Again he clucked his tongue and repeated the soft tap on Doc Holliday's flank, this time easing off a little with the reins to let the horse have his head a little more. For a second it looked as if Doc Holliday would dance sideways again but this time, he moved ahead in an easy walk. Slowly, they walked forward until they came to the end of the corral. Then Clayton eased the reins to the left across the muscular black neck and moved his inside leg forward and outside leg back slightly. The horse took the cue perfectly and turned easily and steadily to the left.

For the next two or three minutes, Clayton walked Doc Holliday around the outer perimeter of the corral, always talking to him, always with just enough pressure on the reins to maintain contact with the horse. Then he executed another left turn, crossed the corral and when they again reached the fence, guided the stallion into a right turn. Again the pair walked around the outside of the corral, this time in the opposite direction. Finally, Clayton eased the horse into one more turn to the right and brought him to a stop in the center of the enclosure.

The seven or eight minutes he had been on Doc's back had been tense ones and now he relaxed a little. Grinning at the small gallery whose attention had been riveted on him and Doc Holliday, he said, "Well, what d'ya think?" He was careful not to raise his voice much. The last thing he wanted to do now was startle the animal after he had performed so well.

"I wouldn't have believed it if I hadn't seen it," Uncle Roy shook his head. "Looks like you passed the test. I think that's probably enough for one day. You'll still have to bring him along slowly."

Clayton nodded and undid the red bandana around his neck to wipe some of the sweat from his face. He hadn't realized how much he had perspired in that short, tension-filled time.

As he passed the cool kerchief over his wet forehead, it slipped from his hand and down in front of Doc Holliday's face. Clayton reached to grab the bandana as it fell. As he did, his hand grazed the top of the stallion's head. It was an automatic reaction and a mistake anyone could have made.

What followed came quickly and gave Clayton no chance to react. The warning yells from the onlookers were too late. Doc Holliday laid back his ears and with a snort leaped ahead. All four of his feet left the ground and when he came down he bunched his back legs as if to kick out but didn't. Nevertheless, the suddenness and power of the move pitched Clayton into a precarious position almost over top of the horse's neck. Doc Holliday followed with one more crow-hop and Clayton was on the ground, flat on his back.

It wasn't the kind of fall that hurt. In fact, it had almost taken place in slow-motion, but there could be no doubt. Although the horse hadn't bucked, at least not hard, he had thrown Clayton to the ground.

When Clayton stood up, there were tears in his eyes. He looked at Doc Holliday, standing a few paces away, acting as if nothing had happened. The boy's anger and hurt erupted. "You stupid idiot!," he screamed at the horse. "What did you do that for? Don't you know what this means?"

Roy jumped down from the fence and crossed to his nephew. Gently, he placed a big hand on the boy's shoulders which were shaking with sobs. "Take it easy, son," Roy told him gently. "You did the best you could. You've got nothing to be ashamed of. And don't be too hard on old Doc. He just couldn't quite get it out of his system."

"But," Clayton began, then stopped. He realized there was no point in arguing. His uncle's warning had been very explicit. Furthermore, it had been fair. He would have to face up to the fact that he had failed. Doc Holliday would continue to be a wild horse and there was nothing that he, Clayton Findlay, could do about it.

His thoughts were interrupted by a yell. From the fence, Aunt Laura shouted, "Roy, I think one of the bulls is out."

Instantly Roy broke away from Clayton, ran to the edge of the corral and peered down the slope to the pen which housed the prized D Lazy D bucking bulls. Sure enough, one of the bulls was out and headed straight west, the worst possible direction. A short distance off in that direction lay the only bad part of the entire spread, sixty acres of gooey bog and heavy brush. If a bull got into it, it might never come out. Worst of all, the bull that was ambling unconcernedly towards that possible fate was Bad Medicine, the bull they could least afford to lose.

117

"I thought you closed the gate," Josh reprimanded his sister.

"I thought you did," Jenny retorted.

"Never mind that, come on!" their father ordered. As he flung the gate of the corral open, Roy yelled back to the others, "We don't have time to get horses. We'll have to try to head him off on foot."

Roy, Josh and Jenny were sprinting hard down the hill. As they ran, Roy gestured toward the bulls' corral and Josh veered off to close the gate before any more of the single-minded beasts could escape. It quickly became obvious that their efforts to run down the bull were going to be futile. They weren't gaining any ground on the massive animal they needed so badly. They could only hope that by some miracle the bull would turn back on its own before it reached the deadly bog.

Still in the corral, Clayton began undoing the cinch on Doc Holliday's saddle. There wasn't much point in his running along with the other three. One more pair of legs wouldn't make any difference. But wait a minute! Maybe there was a way to head of the escaped bull and at the same time win a reprieve for himself and Doc Holliday.

Quickly, Clayton vaulted back into the saddle. There would be no time to ease the horse into action now. If Bad Medicine was to be caught, they would have to go full out. The bull was nearly out of sight already.

In the saddle, the boy paused and looked over at his Aunt Laura who was standing by the gate watching him. An odd thought crossed Clayton's mind. He remembered back a couple of years to the time in school when his class had learned about the painting Mona Lisa and the mysterious smile on

118

the face of the lady in the picture. Looking at his aunt right at that moment, he thought he could see something of the same smile that had been made so famous by the painter Leonardo da Vinci. The look on Laura Douglas' face didn't say yes but it didn't say no either.

Clayton pressed his legs into Doc's sides, tapped the black rump a little harder this time and urged the splendid stallion forward. For a second the horse hesitated as if making up his mind whether to dump his rider on the ground again. But, as much as he loved to buck, Doc also loved to run, and now run he did. Clayton let him go full out.

The most surprised three people in Alberta that morning were Roy Douglas and his son and daughter. About the time they had been ready to give up the chase, their lungs feeling about ready to burst, a boy on a magnificent black horse blazed by them at full gallop. The horse's mane and tail were streaming in the wind.

It was a sight none of them would soon forget.

Swiftly Clayton and Doc Holliday overtook the escapee and made a wide sweeping turn which put them between the bull and his dangerous destination. If Clayton was thrown off now, the situation would be doubly critical, because he would be in the path of the bull. Even an animal like Bad Medicine which was not noted for his viciousness, given that kind of an opportunity, might not pass it up.

Still the youthful rider didn't hesitate. Reining Doc Holliday hard to the right, he swept in close to the bull. Bad Medicine was confused by the new arrivals and slowed down, though he showed he still had designs on continuing his journey in the same direction. Clayton yelled and waved his arms.

119

"Yaaa, Bull, yaa," he hollered, reining the stallion back to the left. Bad Medicine made a ninety degree turn and headed north. Again Clayton pulled the great horse around and once more they headed off the bull. This time the frustrated animal stopped. Then with a disdainful shake of his mighty head, Bad Medicine turned back in the direction he had come from.

The rest was easy. Clayton stayed a short distance behind the bull with Doc Holliday in a steady trot. Several times, Bad Medicine veered slightly one way or the other. Each time Clayton touched his heels to the horse's sides and quickly they had the bull back on course.

A few minutes later, they passed Roy, Josh and Jenny who were still open-mouthed about what they had just seen. "I hope you're not mad, Uncle Roy," Clayton called cheerfully. "It just seemed like the thing to do."

Roy couldn't manage a reply, but the look on his face showed no trace of anger, in fact, far from it. There was surprise, even amazement on the weather-beaten countenance, but to Clayton's relief, anger was the furthest thing from his uncle's mind.

Later, when Doc Holliday had been walked out, brushed and put back in his corral, the family gathered in the kitchen for welcome dishes of ice cream. Aunt Laura had bought Clayton's favorite, Cherry Chocolate, "just in case there was a celebration."

"Boy, did you save our bacon," Josh breathed a heavy sigh of relief. "Letting that bull get out was a real dumb move."

"Well, I guess that makes us even," Clayton replied. "You and Casey bailed me out when I pulled my dumb move that first day with the bulls."

"There's one thing I don't understand," Roy said slowly to his wife who was sitting next to him. "You were right there. Didn't you try to stop him?"

"Well, Dear, not exactly," Laura replied innocently. "You see, there are times when a girl just has to trust her intuition." Looking over at Clayton, she winked and then turning angelically to her husband, she said, "Another dish of ice cream?"

Roy didn't mind a bit that he had just had one put over on him and he led the laughter that followed. It was a laughter that had humor, relief and pride all rolled into it. Meanwhile, out in his corral, a great black horse munched contentedly at a generous quantity of oats.

Chapter Fifteen

Summer rolled into its prime and brought with it a time of relative quiet and peace to the D Lazy D. There were chores, work on the ranch to catch up on, fences to repair and, of course, more rodeos. But all in all, it was a time to relax, enjoy the prairie sun and even catch up on a little reading.

Clayton, eager to learn as much as he could about the west he had despised only a few weeks earlier, took up reading books about the prairies. He read everything from histories about Louis Riel, the Metis hero who was hanged after the Riel Rebellion, to W. 0. Mitchell's *Who Has Seen the Wind*, the prairie classic which came to be his favorite.

Clayton had become completely at home on the ranch and was developing into a capable cowhand as well. He, Josh and Jenny were inseparable whether they were involved in the work of the ranch or enjoying their leisure time. Clayton spent more and more time on the back of Doc Holliday. It wasn't long before the sight of the two of them became as familiar as the mountain peaks off to the west on a clear day.

Late in July there was new reason for excitement and anticipation. The event was an annual affair, a huge barbecue at the ranch of the McKannins. Clayton looked forward to the day of the barbecue with even more anticipation than the other members of the Douglas family as he hadn't seen Cindy since the Stampede. He was hoping the event would provide an opportunity to spend a little time with the pretty barrel racer. He was particularly hopeful that some of that time might be outside the surveillance of his eagle-eyed cousins.

The day of the barbecue dawned clear and warm and held the promise of a hot, dry day. It was the kind of day everyone was getting used to. The summer had provided little in the way of moisture, other than the couple of days during the Stampede and that had been confined to a relatively small area right around the city itself.

Clayton, who not so long before, had hated everything that hinted of wet weather, knew that rain was necessary to the agricultural community he had become an integral part of. He knew too that if rain didn't fall soon, the year would be a financial disaster for the region's farmers and ranchers. Still, he and everyone else was happy that good weather had prevailed for the day of the barbecue.

After a breakfast of pancakes, bacon and cornbread, Clayton sought out his uncle for a serious conversation. He found Uncle Roy in the barn and approached him hesitatingly. Roy regarded the boy silently but with a gleam in his eye. He knew boys well enough to know that, whatever was on Clayton's mind, he was having trouble getting it out.

Clayton kicked at a bale of straw and said without looking at his uncle, "I guess you know how old I am, don't you?"

Uncle Roy nodded and replied, "It's not too hard to remember, since you're the same age as Josh and Jenny. I guess that makes you thirteen."

"Right," Clayton kicked again at the bale. "Of course some guys mature pretty fast," he pointed out. "Some guys are almost men by the time they're thirteen."

"I can't argue with that," Roy concurred, the smile on his face becoming harder to conceal.

"Well, I was just thinking," Clayton began, "...uh...well, I thought...I mean..."

"What's on your mind, son?" Roy interrupted gently.

"Well," Clayton drew his hand over his chin, "I was thinking with this barbecue being such a big event, maybe I ought to scrape off a few of these whiskers. Just to make myself presentable, you understand."

Uncle Roy didn't answer right away, but kicked at the bail a couple of times himself. "I guess you'd be wanting to borrow my razor, is that it?" he asked, suppressing a grin.

"Kind of," Clayton acknowledged, as he shifted his weight first to one foot, then to the other.

"Maybe I better have a closer look at that beard of yours," Uncle Roy said. Clayton walked over to show him the evidence. Roy placed a sun-darkened hand on the boy's face where a gentle crop of blond down indicated real whiskers wouldn't appear for another year or two.

"Yeah, if I was you, I wouldn't want to show up at a social gathering like this one without getting rid of some of that growth first," he agreed. "You'll find my razor and lather in the medicine chest in the bathroom," he told Clayton, who instantly turned and broke for the house. "Try not to take off too much hide," his uncle called to him, and turned with a chuckle back to his work.

Three hours later, the group from the D Lazy D was enjoying the warm afternoon sun in the company of dozens of neighbors and friends at the McKannin barbecue.

Clayton, sporting a couple of band-aids on his chin, had never seen a feast quite like it. Five enormous barbecue ovens were placed strategically in the McKannin backyard, which was only slightly smaller than a football field. Steaks, cooked to individual taste, baked potatoes, beans that had been cooked in molasses and served in massive pots, salads, buns and even hamburgers and hot dogs for the younger guests made up the fabulous menu.

Clayton and Josh made several trips to one particular table where steaming corn on the cob was piled high. Clayton learned that the idea was to place a sharp stick in one end of the corn and then dip the corn into one of the large pickle jars filled with melted butter.

Having finally stuffed himself nearly to the bursting point, Clayton decided it was time to seek out Cindy McKannin. He made a quick stop at a table where enormous helpings of ice cream were being served. With a dish in each hand, he sauntered over to a tree covered knoll. Cindy was sitting alone in the shade beneath the trees. She was wearing a soft coral-colored dress with puffed up shoulders. A white ribbon in her hair perfectly accented her dark brown hair. To Clayton, Cindy looked prettier than she ever had.

"Oh hi," Clayton tried to make his voice sound as if seeing the girl was the biggest surprise of his life. "Would it be okay if I sat here?" he indicated a patch of grass next to Cindy.

"Sure," Cindy smiled at him.

"Like some ice cream? I've got an extra dish," Clayton offered.

"Okay, thanks," she replied.

Clayton sat down and was just beginning to enjoy the moment when he and Cindy were rather boisterously joined by Jenny and Josh. Clayton tried not to show his disappointment as the twins plopped themselves down for what gave every indication of being a long stay.

"This looks like a nice shady spot," Jenny declared, as she made herself comfortable.

Even the usually reserved Josh couldn't resist a little dig of his own. "Sure glad we came across you two," he said with a grin. "We just couldn't find a place to sit anywhere."

"I bet," Clayton mumbled under his breath.

"How do you like my dress?" Jenny asked bluntly. "I look pretty great, right?"

Had Clayton been in a better frame of mind, he might have agreed that his cousin did, indeed look "pretty great." As it was, however, he replied instead, "From a distance maybe."

Not to be denied, Jenny shook her head. "Oh, no, you're wrong, Cousin, Dad said the dress brings out the color of my eyes, don't you agree?" She leaned forward to allow Clayton a better opportunity to see for himself the dazzling effect of the dress on her eyes.

Suddenly she jerked up straight. "What's that horrible smell?" she demanded. She leaned close to Clayton, then suddenly leaped to her feet. "Geez, you've got Dad's after-shave on.

Clayton's neck and face took on the color of a bottle of ketchup. "Well, just a little," he admitted.

"A little!" Jenny scoffed. "You smell like you had a bath in the stuff. Yuk!"

Clayton tried to stammer out a reply, but was mercifully spared the effort when Ben Bradley propped himself against a tree not far away. The cowboy began strumming a battered old guitar and singing softly. Soon a cluster of people gathered around Ben. Some were humming or singing along while others just basked in the warmth of the day and relaxed after the supper.

It was a side of Ben Clayton had never seen and he was surprised at how well the rugged cowboy sang and played. Ben had a gentle, baritone voice and he sang the old songs, cowboy songs like "Streets of Laredo," "Bury Me Not on the Lone Prairie" and "The Old Chisholm Trail." When one of the guests called "How about a Wilf Carter number"? Ben nodded and went into a pretty good imitation of the west's favorite minstrel in a song called "Strawberry Roan." Clayton could almost visualize scenes exactly like this one taking place a hundred years earlier as the pioneers rested during the backbreaking and sometimes heartbreaking task of opening and settling the west.

In answer to another request from one of his listeners, Ben had just begun to sing "Don't Fence Me In" when attention was diverted to a rapidly approaching pick-up truck. The truck raced up the roadway toward the picnickers and slammed to a stop just a few feet from where Ben was entertaining. The driver, a man Clayton had seen before but didn't know, leaped from the cab of the truck and shouted, "Roy! Roy Douglas!"

Roy was among the group listening to Ben. He had been lying with his head on his wife's lap, drifting in and out of a peaceful sleep. Now he was wide awake, on his feet in an instant, and quickly approached the new arrival.

"What's wrong, Cy?" he demanded.

"Prairie fire. Your place. In the northwest pasture. The wind's carrying it toward Hector's cabin," came the staccato reply.

Immediately, every head turned toward the D Lazy D, off to the north, and every eye saw the tell-tale black smoke winding skyward.

"Let's go," Roy shouted, and in minutes the grounds were virtually deserted as the picnickers scrambled into their vehicles and raced to combat the deadly menace.

Prairie fire!

Chapter Sixteen

Clayton rode with Josh and Uncle Roy. On the way he heard the story of Hector Levy.

"You remember that first morning you were at the ranch and while you were helping Dad load bulls, I was out checking fences? Dad told me to check on Hector and see how he was," Josh reminded his cousin.

"Yeah, now that you mention it, I do remember hearing the name," Clayton replied.

"Right, well, Hector is kind of a legend in these parts," Josh went on. "I guess you'd call him a hermit. He's been living up in our north pasture for about fifteen years now, right Dad?"

Roy nodded in confirmation, his eyes remaining glued to the road as he raced the truck toward the ranch.

"Some people think he's crazy and I guess other folks think he's hiding out," Josh continued.

"But the truth is he's neither of those things," Roy interjected. "Hector Levy was a rodeo cowboy, one of the best bronc riders I ever saw. He rode the ones nobody else could ride and scored high on 'em to boot. One day there was a robbery not far from here. A hardware store was held up and the proprietor was wounded," Roy went on grimly. "At first there didn't appear to be any clues. Then somebody said they had seen Hector in the vicinity just a few hours before the holdup. Pretty soon a whole bunch of people were claiming they had seen Hector at the hardware store at the exact time of the crime.

"Then, to top it all off, the store proprietor who all along had said he didn't see the robber, changed his mind and stated publicly that it was Hector Levy who shot him, which was quite a turn around since he had been shot in the back. Hector was convicted and sent to prison. He was in there for three years when a guy who had been arrested for a couple of other robberies confessed to this one." Roy's anger had been mounting as he recounted the story and now he paused to take a deep breath.

"When Hector came back looking for a job, nobody wanted to give him one. I guess folks found it a little embarrassing having him around. There was an old cabin in our north pasture that nobody was using. Hector asked if he could use it for a little while. He's been there ever since and he's welcome to stay for the rest of his life. He grows a few vegetables and has some chickens and he gets by all right. He keeps to himself and doesn't trust anyone so you won't find him friendly," Roy concluded.

"I guess I can't blame him for that, after what happened," Clayton stated thoughtfully.

The truck was approaching the edge of the fire. Clayton had never seen anything like it. As far as he could see to the north, the fire's blazing tentacles, aided by a strong wind, licked at the tinder dry grass and shrubs. Behind the fire an enormous black blanket of waste lay where the flames had already been. Off to the left in the path of the fire, a cabin stood perched on a gentle rise. Clayton knew that must be Hector's place.

Then he saw the strangest sight of all. One man, all alone, his face blackened by smoke and heat from the fire, his long hair and beard shining in the fire's glow, stood at the edge of the blaze, beating furiously with gunny sacks at the ever-encroaching flames. That man, Clayton knew instinctively, was

Hector Levy, fighting to save what little he had left in the world.

Instantly, the small army of neighbors leaped from the vehicles and entered the battle. Roy assumed command and quickly improvised a strategy for fighting the blaze. Ben Bradley and Jack McKannin, Cindy's father, were dispatched to the nearest farmhouses to try and commandeer a tractor or two.

About fifteen men with shovels set to work clearing a firebreak just in front of Hector's cabin. The break was to be as wide as they could make it and would go as far as the men could get cleared before the fire got that far. If Ben and Mr. McKannin succeeded in borrowing tractors, they would be used as well to create the firebreak.

Laura Douglas organized a number of women and older children into a bucket brigade to carry water from the well, situated precariously close to the fire, to douse the outside walls of the frail cabin. This was a tough side of his aunt which Clayton hadn't seen before. For a moment he stood mesmerized, watching as she transformed the group of gentle, easy-going farm people into a determined, well-organized human chain with buckets moving from hand-to-hand with factory speed and precision. At the cabin, Jenny and Cindy, their party dresses already in shambles, were throwing bucket after bucket against the cabin walls.

The rest of the gallant band of firefighters, including Josh and Clayton, joined Hector at the edge of the fire, beating, stamping and throwing earth on the flames. They knew their efforts could not stop the relentless advance of the fire but they hoped they could slow it down enough to allow sufficient time for the break to be cleared.

For an hour they fought with every ounce of their strength, always having to fall back before the cruel heat and searing smoke of the fire. Now there was precious little ground between them and the group of men working furiously to create the break. In spite of their heroic efforts, Clayton could see that the break wasn't wide enough or long enough. The fire would jump it easily and carry on unimpeded to Hector's cabin.

Then, just when it looked like there was no chance left, Ben Bradley could be seen rumbling across the field at the wheel of a mammoth green tractor. Behind him came Mr. McKannin on a second, slightly smaller version of the first. Both tractors were packed with people, perched on fenders and hanging on grimly to the sides of the wildly bouncing machines. Here were reinforcements for the exhausted band of people that had been fighting the fire.

The new arrivals leaped from the tractors and fell on the leading edge of the fire with a vengeance. Those who had been near exhaustion, encouraged by the much needed help, found new energy and redoubled their efforts. Behind them, the two tractors swiftly widened the existing break, at the same time creating a mound of earth behind the break to block the progress of the fire.

Every minute counted as the tractors, at the experienced hands of Ben and Mr. McKannin, roared up and down, lengthening, widening and deepening the firebreak. But would it be enough? Soon they would know if their efforts were in vain. The fire had reached the break.

"Clayton and Josh," Roy called, "get up on the roof of the cabin and beat out any sparks that hit up there."

The battle raged on. Roy gathered all his people on the cabin side of the break, and side by side the firefighters beat down flames and places where sparks from the prairie fire were igniting smaller blazes. On the roof of the cabin, Josh and Clayton pounced back and forth, hurling themselves on every spark that landed there.

For a while it seemed that neither side was gaining an advantage. The fire was stopped for the moment but it wasn't diminishing. Meanwhile, the firefighters had stopped the progress of the flames, but they were tiring as the long hours of backbreaking toil in the intense heat had taken their toll. It was doubtful whether they could hold out much longer.

Through it all Hector Levy had not spoken a word. It was as though he hadn't noticed the arrival of the dozens of men, women and young people who were trying to save his modest home. He fought on, rarely looking either to the right or the left, his attention riveted on the fire in front of him.

Then, Ben yelled, "The wind's shifting!" And sure enough, it was. With dusk approaching, the wind, which had been the fire's chief ally was lessening and changing directions. Within a half hour the flames were being blown back toward the already burned ground. With no new grass to feed it, the fire began to die out. By evening, all that remained was an enormous piece of charred prairie, smoke still rising from the blackened earth. And at the edge of the burned-over area, the ramshackle cabin still stood.

The bedraggled army of firefighters dropped exhaustedly to the ground, at first unable to move or even speak. Gradually life returned to aching limbs and flagging spirits rose again. Soon there was conversation, quiet at first, then more boisterous and accompanied by laughing. The sound of laughter—excited, proud, relieved laughter—could be heard rolling over the scorched prairie.

Finally, it was as if the McKannin barbecue had moved lock, stock and barrel to the grassy knoll behind Hector Levy's cabin. Someone hauled a guitar out of the back of a pick-up truck and Ben, still perched on the tractor, looking to Clayton like a blackened knight on a mechanical charger, led the second half of the interrupted singsong.

After Ben had finished one song, Hector Levy stood up and said simply, "I want to thank all of you." There were tears in his eyes. That day, the old man that some people called crazy, had won the fight to save a worn-out old cabin, and along the way had gained some friends, something he hadn't had for just about fifteen years.

Still, several questions remained. How had the fire started that warm summer's day? Had it been a natural occurrence? With almost all of the local residents at the McKannin's barbecue, it would have been a simple matter for a culprit to set the fire and escape undetected. Had it not been for the determined work of good neighbors, and a fortunate change in the wind, Hector Levy's cabin and most of the D Lazy D hay crop would have been gone. The wind had certainly blown in their favor, at least for the time being.

Chapter Seventeen

Less than a week after the prairie fire, rain finally came to the parched land. It was the first major rain of the summer. Almost overnight, brown grass turned green, leaves recaptured their lost color, and soil that had been little more than dust and cracks became a place where crops could again grow and ripen.

The rodeo season continued on in high gear. Clayton and his adopted family were on the road much of the time, the familiar blue and gold painted stock trucks of the D Lazy D announcing the revival of the Old West to town after town.

Clayton, like most eastern visitors to the west, was particularly taken by the quaint and colorful names of some of the communities. He looked forward to telling everyone back home that he had actually visited the place called Medicine Hat. Clayton, Josh and Jenny had been planning a surprise, a big surprise. They decided the time to spring it was at the Medicine Hat Stampede.

The rodeo in Medicine Hat began on a Thursday afternoon and it was then that Roy learned with a jolt what Clayton and his ever-willing cousins had been plotting. It happened as Roy was looking over the draw sheet, where all of the contestants for the entire rodeo were listed. He noted that Josh would be riding on Saturday afternoon and then almost fell over. Right below his son's name was the name of Clayton Findlay.

A few minutes later he found the two boys sipping cokes next to Tub Willoughby's motor home. "What's going on here?" he asked waving the draw sheet in front of them and struggling to keep his voice under control.

"What do you mean, Dad?" Josh asked innocently.

"You know what I mean," his father answered. "Look, Clayton, I think it's great that you want to try riding steers but this isn't the best place to start. The steers here will be tough. You could get hurt. Now if you want to learn to ride steers, you practice a bunch at the ranch and maybe we'll get you on one at a rodeo a little later on."

"We've been doing that," Clayton responded.

"What?" Roy's eyes showed his surprise.

"It's true, Dad. Clayton has been practicing for almost a month now," Jenny confirmed.

"And I'm not doing too bad. I can ride those practice steers about four out of five times now," Clayton added. "Josh scores my rides and says they're getting better all the time."

"Is that true, Josh?" Roy asked his son.

"It sure is, Dad," the boy answered earnestly. "He's improved a lot since he started. Clayton knows the steer he rides here is going to be tougher than what he's used to at home, but I think he's ready. Anyway, a cowboy has to try the tough ones sometime, doesn't he?"

Roy took off his cowboy hat and scratched his head. Then he looked at the three young people whose eyes were glued to his face. "You guys put up a pretty good argument," he acknowledged, a slow smile spreading over his rugged features. "All right, young fella," he said to Clayton, "I can't say I'm not proud of you for wanting to try. Good luck," Roy clapped his nephew on the shoulder.

Instantly Josh stood up and tossed his hat into the air as Jenny whooped her excitement. Clayton sat back, took another drink of coke and grinned at his uncle. But his mind was already racing three days ahead to his first ride.

The first two days of the Medicine Hat Stampede were a blur in Clayton's memory and few of the details of them stood out. In what seemed like no time at all, Saturday arrived and with it the tension of a cowboy's first competition. During the first few events of the rodeo, Clayton listened to Josh's quiet voice coolly and confidently offering advice. "This is no different than at the ranch," his cousin had told him. "So just ride the same way you do there."

It was soon time for the Boys' Steer Riding. Josh was second man out. He scored a 76, third best of the rodeo so far and probably good enough to win at least a portion of the prize money.

Clayton was to be the last rider and would be coming out of chute five. With three contestants to go, he and Josh dropped the rope and cowbell that hung from it around the steer's back, bringing it around and looping it through and up the other side.

Now it was just a matter of waiting for his turn. Clayton straddled the chute above the steer and watched the last two riders go. Then the chute boss, whose job it was to help the stock contractor keep the rodeo moving along, pointed to Clayton and barked, "You're next. Get down on him."

Clayton was vaguely aware of the familiar voice of Hank Parker telling the crowd that this was the first official ride for the next cowboy, all the way from Toronto, Ontario. As he heard his own name over the public address system, Clayton realized there was no turning back. What surprised him was the realization that he had no desire to turn away from the challenge facing him. He was actually looking forward to this moment. He wanted to do it, for Josh and Jenny, for his uncle and most of all, for himself.

It was a bigger steer than he was used to. Clayton was surprised at the width of the animal as he carefully lowered himself down onto its back. He felt a bit uneasy but was reassured when he looked up to see his Uncle Roy drop down into the chute at the steer's head. "Now take a good wrap on this steer. Nobody is going to rush you. Just take your time and nod your head when you're good and ready," his uncle said. "Don't forget, anybody who can tame a wild horse, can doggone sure ride one of these."

As Clayton slipped his gloved hands into the handhold, Josh pulled on the free end of the rope making it tight. Then he passed the rope through Clayton's open palms, around his wrists and once more into his hands. Clayton forced his hands closed, the fingers of his gloves forming a determined grip around the rope.

"Now slide forward so you're sitting right up against your rope," Uncle Roy told him. Clayton followed his uncle's instructions and the steer tensed and tried to jerk as it reacted to the movement on its back.

Roy said quietly, "Now remember to sit up, and stick your chest out. Don't let yourself get thrown forward over his head. And watch your stock. Look at his head as you're riding him. A lot of times you can tell which way he is going to go. Now, are you ready?"

"Yeah," whispered Clayton, hoarsely.

"All right, when you want them to open the chute gate just nod your head," Roy said.

Clayton looked up at him briefly and saw his uncle's encouraging smile. Then he looked back down at the steer, gritted his teeth and nodded his head. For a second nothing happened as the man on the chute gate, having seen the nod, jerked the handle up on the gate and swung it open. Roy forced the steer's head around toward the open gate.

All at once, things began to happen very quickly. The steer's first jump was a high one and as it came down on its front legs, it kicked out at the back, in classic bucking style. For two more jumps it looked as if Clayton had been born to ride steers. He sat up as his uncle had directed and hung on with grim determination. Then suddenly the steer, while in mid air, contorted its body into a left turn and when it came down was into a spin. Still Clayton was able to maintain his balance aboard the spinning and bucking steer. Then the animal, in another unpredictable move, came out of the spin as quickly as it had gone into it, leaping high and crashing to the earth hard on its front feet, its back almost perpendicular to the a ground. That jump had thrown Clayton back off his rope and slightly to one side. As Clayton tried to recover, the steer catapulted into still another high jump, kicking out its back legs in mid air. The steer and rider both hit the it ground at the same time, the boy landing hard on his left shoulder and turning in a complete somersault, just an instant before the horn sounded. Roy and Josh sprang into action. Running from the chutes, they arrived at Clayton's side as he was slowly trying to get up.

"Just take it easy," Roy said. "We'll give you a hand."

"How close was I?" Clayton asked, shaking his head to clear the cobwebs.

"Must have been seven seconds, sure as I'm standing here," Josh grinned. "That was one heck of a try."

"You okay?" Roy asked, his face showing his concern.

"Sure," Clayton nodded and a smile of pride came over his face.

"You did fine, just fine," his uncle added as he handed the youngster his hat.

Clayton stood up on his own and walked slowly back towards the chutes. Clint Runner was standing at the chute looking at him.

"Good ride," he told Clayton. "Nobody could've done any better."

He turned and started walking away.

"Clint," Clayton called. "Wait a second." Clint turned slowly to face him, "Uh.... I just wanted to tell you. I've been thinking it over and I don't think I'd mind being called C. J. I mean, if you still think it's a good idea."

"Well," Clint smiled, "you sure have earned it now. So long C. J."

There hadn't been any real need to rush home so the Douglas outfit remained in Medicine Hat overnight. The next morning, a mood of relaxed satisfaction at a job well done prevailed as the family went about the business of loading the stock and preparing for the journey home. By just after ten o'clock, the two liners, followed by Laura Douglas at the wheel of the camper, were on their way back to the D Lazy D.

In the cab of the first liner, Josh and Clayton recounted the tense seconds of their rides. Recounted and recounted and recounted! Finally after the twelfth telling, Ben looked at the two boys from

140

behind the wheel and said, "You know, to listen to you two bandits, anybody'd think you were old-time cowboys. The yarns get wilder each time you tell `em."

Both boys responded with cries of protest at the good-natured admonition, but each had to admit there was probably something in what Ben had said. From that point on, they toned down their stories — but only a little.

The hours tend to pass more quickly when the travellers making those hours are in a festive mood. The trip from Medicine Hat back to the ranch seemed to go by in the wink of an eye. It was still mid-afternoon when the first liner, with Ben at the wheel and Josh and Clayton alongside, pulled slowly into the yard.

Instantly, the feeling of joviality that had been so much in evidence changed to one of apprehension. No one could say why but there was an immediate sense that something was wrong — terribly wrong.

They were met at the gate by Nathan Fuller, the neighbor Roy hired to look after chores while the Douglases were away at rodeos. Standing just off the road, the short, powerfully-built man, a few years older than either Roy or Bradley, held up an arm to signal the truck to stop. Ben braked the huge rig to a slow, lurching halt and rolled down the window.

"Howdy, Nathan," he called over the noise of the truck. "What's up?"

"I'm afraid it's not too good, Ben," came the grim reply. He looked at Josh and said, "It's your dog, son."

"Casey?" Josh cried out.

Instantly the truck cab emptied. By that time, the second liner had pulled in behind the first and Roy and Jenny, sensing that something was out of the ordinary, had hurried forward to join the group.

"What's wrong with Casey?" Josh asked, terrified at what might be the answer.

"What's happened to him?" Clayton questioned, his voice too showing alarm.

"Somebody shot him, near as I can figger," Nathan shook his head sadly. "Leastways, that's what it looks like. He's bleedin' awful bad."

"Is he alive?" Jenny managed between muffled sobs.

"Yes, Ma'am, he is," Nathan nodded, "but I'm afraid he hasn't got a chance. I was just about to end his suffering when you..."

"Where is he?" Josh interrupted in a barely audible voice.

"Right up by the house," Nathan pointed. Instantly the whole family, including Laura Douglas, who had arrived just in time to hear the end of the conversation, bolted for the house.

There, at the foot of the steps leading up to the front door, the crumpled form of Casey lay. He was on his side and next to him a large patch of grass was stained red with the dog's blood. Seeing the approach of the people he loved, Casey valiantly tried to wag his tail. It moved only slightly. The once clear, mischievous eyes were clouded with pain and bewilderment.

Jenny dropped beside Casey, and buried her face in the dog's long hair, her shoulders shaking with grief. Clayton knelt next to her and gently placed his hand near the ugly, angry wound where the blood was starting to congeal and mat Casey's yellow-brown hair. Josh, too, bent near his long-time companion and friend. He gently

142

ran a hand over the familiar head. Tears streamed unchecked down the two boys' faces. Behind them stood Roy and Laura Douglas, the color drained from their faces.

Each had a personal recollection of the dog that had often seemed more human than canine. For Roy and his wife, it was the skunk encounter that had sent the luckless Casey, after receiving the full force of the spray, into a frenzied run round and round the house. Apparently he hoped to be able to outrun the offending stench. At the time, the hilarity of the dog's pitiful plight had brought tears of laughter streaming down the faces of the Douglas family. Now the whole episode, including the almost impossible task of bathing the unfortunate dog in tomato juice that followed, was only a sad reminiscence, to be smiled at through tears of sorrow.

For Josh, his fondest memory of Casey involved the countless hours he and the energetic dog spent in riding the hills and valleys of the D Lazy D, checking fences, collecting stray cows and occasionally visiting Hector Levy.

Jenny's fondest memories were of Casey's puppyhood. Jenny had spent much of that summer three years ago on the back porch reading the "Anne" novels. Often, as she did, a tiny bundle of yellow fluff would snuggle into her lap and fall contentedly asleep in the summer sun.

For his part, Clayton recalled that infamous day at the bulls' corral when Casey had saved Uncle Roy from serious injury from the hooves and horns of the vicious Little Bighorn. It was that same courage and loyalty that today would cost the dog his life.

There was no question of saving him and each of them realized it. Jenny asked the one question on all their minds. "Why?" she sobbed bitterly.

Nathan Fuller approached slowly. "Way I see it," he rubbed a hand over a bewhiskered chin, "somebody had to be trying to get into the house for some reason. Casey here, must've been protectin' the place like he should and they up and shot him.

"But you know somethin'... whoever it was didn't get in," the hired man went on. "Even with that bullet in him, he must've scared 'em off. There's blood up and down the stairs like he'd been up there guardin' the door and no one's been inside the house; I looked.

"I figure he was probably layin' there for maybe two hours b'fore I got here," Nathan continued. "And when he heard me comin', he tried to get back up the stairs again to stand guard. There ain't many dogs better than that one, I'll guarantee you."

"There's none better than Casey," Josh amended with fierce pride.

For a moment, the six people stood or knelt next to the dog that had never looked like much but had a heart as big as the ranch he had loved to roam. And for each the grief was matched only by rage and frustration. Why had such a senseless, callous thing happened? Who would strike down the happy, fun-loving dog who had only been doing his duty?

Casey let out a soft, low moan, his first and only indication of the pain that had to be racking his body.

"I know it would be hard for you folks," Nathan Fuller said softly, "so if you want, I can put him out of his misery."

144

But Casey, who had kept death at bay for so long, hoping for one last glimpse of the masters he loved and had served so faithfully, could wait no more. With an almost whispered sigh, the gallant dog closed his eyes.

"That won't be necessary, Mr. Fuller," sobbed Josh, "our dog just died."

Chapter Eighteen

Whoever had shot Casey had left no clues. The R.C.M.P. investigated the incident but could find nothing to indicate who the culprit or culprits might have been. No one in the area had seen anything out of the ordinary that day and the police were unable to turn up any clearly defined tire tracks or footprints.

They agreed with Nathan Fuller's theory that it had probably been thieves, and that Casey had foiled their attempt to get into the house. When the faithful dog refused to back down from the criminals, they shot him. Then, afraid that the sound of the shot might attract attention from neighbors, they had fled, leaving Casey to bleed to death. Eventually, the police had informed the Douglases that unless and until some new information or evidence was uncovered, they were forced to abandon their investigation.

The next few weeks dragged agonizingly as it seemed to everyone that a member of the family was gone. Casey's welcoming bark, the enthusiastic wag of his tail, and the funny habit he had of scurrying back and forth between them when they arrived back at the D Lazy D from a rodeo, would never again be a part of their lives. Still, hard as it was to carry on normally, there was no choice. There was a ranch to be looked after, lives to be led and, as always, the rodeo road to be travelled.

The end of summer approached. As the days gradually grew shorter and the nights began to take on their autumn chill, the professional rodeo season too, wound down. It was time for the last regular rodeo of this year, one of over fifty that would lead up to the season finale at the Canadian Finals Rodeo.

The last regular season stop for the D Lazy D would be at Morley, an Indian community situated half way between the Douglas ranch and the mighty mountains to the west. Both liners had been loaded, everyone was ready to go and Roy was pacing up and down in front of one of the trucks. The usually reliable Ben Bradley was late.

Roy had phoned Ben's house and had been told by Mrs. Bradley that her husband hadn't returned yet from a rodeo at Saskatoon, Saskatchewan but that he had phoned to say he would be going directly to the D Lazy D. There was nothing to do but wait. It wasn't like Ben to be late, and since he hadn't phoned Roy, he must be on his way.

Roy was still pacing not long afterward when the familiar sight of Ben's pick-up truck turned into the driveway of the ranch. A minute later, Ben was out of the cab and receiving a cup of coffee from Laura Douglas. He responded with a grateful nod and turned to Roy.

"Sorry I'm late Roy but there were big goings-on in Saskatchewan," he explained.

"What kind of goings-on?" Roy inquired.

"It looks like our rodeo marauder has struck again," Ben informed him.

"You're kidding," exclaimed Roy and instantly Josh, Jenny and Clayton, who had all been loafing against the rail of a fence, pressed closer to hear the details.

"What happened?" they asked almost in unison.

"This was the worst yet," Ben began. "There were three performances at the rodeo and something happened at all three. During the first performance a roper and bulldogger both had to pull up during their runs. At first it looked like their horses were injured 'cause they came up limping. But it turned out that both had thrown shoes. Afterwards it looked as if somebody must have tampered with those shoes."

"Why would anybody do something like that?" Josh wondered out loud.

"Why would anybody do *any* of the things that have happened?" Roy mused.

"That was just the start of the problems," continued Ben. "During the second performance two guys had their ropes stolen. They turned up in a garbage can after the rodeo, but they had to use borrowed ropes for their runs which was a disadvantage and neither of them had good times. Then just before the final performance our old friend Lefty Shivers had his horse stolen."

Ben Bradley chuckled and shook his head, "I know it's not funny, but I'll guarantee you I have never seen anybody that mad in my life. I thought he was going to burst, he was so red in the face."

"Did they get the horse back?" Roy asked his friend.

"Afraid not, Roy," Ben replied, no longer laughing, "We formed a search party just like we did in Taber but we couldn't turn up any sign of the horse."

"Sounds like the rodeo was a bit of a disaster," Roy Douglas noted.

"Yeah, about the only good news was that Len Tucker won the Roping and the All-Round there. That means Len and Lefty Shivers are just about tied for the All-Round Championship for the year," Ben concluded.

"Hey, wouldn't it be great if Len could finally finish first?" Clayton chipped in.

Roy looked thoughtful.

148

"Got an idea who the culprit might be, Roy?" Ben asked him.

"Wish I did," Roy replied. "I would have been willing to bet Lefty Shivers was involved in some way, but I guess this'll have to change my thinking."

"Unless he victimized himself to throw suspicion away from him," Ben suggested.

Roy shook his head, "I don't think he'd do that if it meant missing out on a chance to win a rodeo, especially with the race for the All-Round Champion so close," he pointed out.

"Yeah, I guess you're right," Ben nodded in agreement.

"Well, let's hit the road," Roy said. "We've got a rodeo of our own to get to."

Morley was one of the most important rodeos of the year as competitors strove to make good on this last opportunity to qualify for the Canadian Finals. For this trip, Clayton rode in the cab of one liner with Ben while Roy and Josh rode in the other. Laura and Jenny followed in the family camper. Conversation in all three vehicles focused on the series of mysteries that continued to plague the rodeo circuit. Everyone had a theory. Ben thought it was a gang of people working from outside rodeo to harm the sport. He admitted he could think of no reason that anybody not in the sport would take the trouble to damage and steal equipment and animals, but he refused to believe that the crimes were being committed by any of his fellow cowboys.

Clayton disagreed. He figured that Miles Shivers, the bullying younger brother of Lefty Shivers was probably involved in some way, even though Lefty's horse was the latest to disappear. In the other liner, Josh held to the theory that it was Lefty himself who was behind the many incidents and that he had staged stealing his own horse to throw off suspicion.

Roy, meanwhile, was tight-lipped as to his own thoughts on the subject, though he did admit to his son that he was convinced that the culprit or culprits had to be someone either involved in rodeo or close enough to it to know the detailed movements of the competitors.

Then, too, there were all of the unexplained misfortunes that had beset the D Lazy D. In the camper, Jenny and her mother focused their attention on that aspect of the puzzle, but neither could offer any solid explanation or even guess whether they were in some way related to the latest rash of mysterious incidents.

Once at the rodeo grounds, however, all was forgotten in the business of readying the arena and stock for the upcoming rodeo. Josh and Jenny were both scheduled to compete on the first night and Clayton was up during the last performance.

In addition, Len Tucker, good friend of all of them, had drawn Bad Medicine for his bull ride on the final day. If ever there was a case of mixed emotions, that was it. As much as everyone connected with the D Lazy D wanted to see the great bull's perfect record of never having been ridden continue, there wasn't one of them that wished the hard-luck, perennial runner-up cowboy anything but success.

The first performance was highlighted by two incidents. Rodeo clown Tub Willoughby and the announcer Hank Parker were continuing their usual exchange of insults, which always delighted the crowd when suddenly the portly clown threw a bucket of water into the announcer's stand, thoroughly dousing the popular man behind the microphone. Probably for the first time in his career, Hank Parker was stuck for words.

When he recovered himself, the announcer promised over the microphone to get revenge on Tub Willoughby who had, by that time, gone up into the crowd and was hiding behind a very pretty blond woman. Needless to say, the rodeo fans were loving every minute of the antics of the two men, who were, in fact, old friends.

The other outstanding feature of that first performance at Morley was provided by none other than Josh himself as he scored a sensational 83 points in the Boys' Steer Riding. That effort easily gave him the lead after one day of competition, but Clayton quickly pointed out to his cousin that his lead would surely be erased when he made his own ride during the third and final performance.

Actually, Clayton had been on four more steers in competition since his debut at Medicine Hat. While he had ridden two of them, he had yet to score high enough to be "in the money."

"Too bad, Josh," he kidded his cousin, "I know you can use the cash, but I'm afraid I'm just going to have to beat you."

"I just hope we don't need a shovel to dig you out of the dirt when you fall off," Josh returned the jibe.

Jenny's run in the barrel racing was smooth but not fast enough as many of the best cowgirls in the world were entered at Morley.

The second day also passed without a hitch. It looked as if the rodeo marauder, who had been so busy at the Saskatoon rodeo, had taken a holiday.

For the final performance of the Morley rodeo and the season, the smell of autumn was rich in the mountain air. The leaves that for some time had been turning their various shades of red, orange and yellow, were now beginning to fall from their lofty summer perches to form a technicolor blanket over the land. The signs of impending winter were everywhere.

During breakfast in the Douglas camper, Jenny joked about the fact that two of the family "stars," Bad Medicine and Clayton were both appearing in the same performance.

"I know one thing," Clayton responded. "If Bad Medicine is as psyched up as I am, Len Tucker is going to have his hands full." Breakfast was barely completed when there was a light tap on the door of the camper.

"Come on in," Roy called out.

The door opened and Clint Runner shyly poked his head inside. The Indian boy did not enter. "I was wondering if you were busy this morning," he addressed Jenny.

"Not all that busy, I guess," Jenny responded, a little puzzled. "What's up?"

"Nothing really," Clint replied. "But if you've got a few minutes, there's something I'd like you to see. Morning," he added by way of general greeting to the rest of the camper's occupants.

"Okay," the girl replied with a look at her dad to see if it was all right that she accompany their unexpected visitor. Roy nodded approval.

"Just me?" Jenny queried with a little giggle.

"If that's okay," was the answer.

"Well, let's go then." With a toss of her red curls, Jenny followed Clint out of the camper. The door slammed shut behind them leaving four somewhat bewildered people inside.

Quickly, however, attention was diverted to other activities. Clayton helped his aunt clean up from breakfast while Josh and Roy attacked the paper work that was a distasteful but necessary part of every rodeo.

The help had to be paid and cheques written to cover wages. As well, Roy kept meticulous records on how the stock bucked at each performance. Josh helped him record the scores given each of the D Lazy D animals through the first two performances at Morley. Roy and Josh also jotted down a few notes about the stock scheduled to buck today. Those notes would be given to Hank Parker, the Rodeo Announcer, to assist him in keeping the crowd advised on what to look for during the rodeo.

Once the breakfast cleanup was complete, Laura joined Roy and Josh to help with the paper work, while Clayton stretched out on the top bunk with a copy of *To Kill a Mockingbird* which he was reading for Language Arts.

About an hour later, there was another tap on the door, this one even softer than the first. Josh crossed to the door and opened it. There was Jenny, hunched over and backing into the camper! It looked as if she might be hurt and Josh stepped closer to give her a hand.

"Get back!" she ordered. "Right back. Stay right there." Josh did as he was told and stepped back to the kitchen table. Jenny was still standing with her back to them, although she had now straightened up.

Suddenly she turned around. There cradled in her arms was the cutest tangle of legs, tail and floppy ears any of them had ever seen. The pup looked around through unsure brown eyes as Jenny placed it on the kitchen table, right in the middle of her father's pile of papers. The puppy's tiny tail began to wag, reluctantly at first, then with as much speed as the miniature backside could muster.

"Where did you get him?" Josh asked incredulously.

"He's a present for us," Jenny replied triumphantly. "From Clint Runner and his family. They heard about Casey and wondered if we'd like a pup. Their dog had a litter about six weeks ago. What do you think? Isn't he cute?"

Clayton spoke the words that were on all of their tongues. "He looks just like a miniature Casey."

"I know," Jenny turned serious. "That's why I picked him out of the litter. Can we keep him, Dad?"

Instantly all eyes were on Roy. For a minute he looked thoughtful. "Well, I don't know. The thing that worries me the most is..." Here he paused and stroked his chin reflectively.

"What?" the three youngsters chorused in unison.

"...Is this." He continued slowly, enjoying the near agony on the expectant faces. "If you don't get him off my papers, he could have an accident, and that wouldn't be a good way for a new family dog to get acquainted."

As Josh and Clayton cheered, Jenny hastily scooped the bewildered pup off the table and onto the floor.

"Oh, there's just one little thing," Jenny said hesitatingly. "He's a she."

"Oh no," Josh groaned. "Pretty soon we're going to be outnumbered by females in this family."

154

"Geez, you're not kidding," Clayton agreed, a pained expression on his face.

"Now just a minute!" Jenny flared, but stopped when the two boys broke into laughter and bent down to extend greetings to the newest member of the Douglas family.

"What'll we call her?" Josh mused, running a hand over the pup's scruffy yellow coat.

"I think we should call her Casey," Jenny announced to everyone's surprise.

"Don't you think that might bring back unpleasant memories?" her mother wondered aloud.

"And besides," Josh argued, "Casey's a boy's name — Casey Jones, Casey Stengel... you can't give her a boy's name."

"Boys, schmoys," Jenny huffed. "Who says you can't?"

"I like the idea," Clayton put in. "I don't think we'd have unpleasant memories, Aunt Laura. I think they'd be pleasant ones."

"You might be right at that," his aunt nodded agreement.

Josh picked up the puppy and peered into the enormous, sad eyes. "How do you feel about it?" he asked the tiny dog. "What do you think of the name Casey?" As if to reply, the pup squirmed happily and gave the boy's hand a moist lick. Josh laughed and said "Well, I guess that settles it. Casey it is."

"There is one thing I don't quite understand," Roy pondered aloud as he looked at the pup in Josh's arms. "I wonder how Clint Runner got wind of what happened to Casey. It's not something any of us had talked about to many people."

"Oh, you know how news travels, Dad," Jenny replied quickly. "He must have heard it somewhere.

Actually there are a lot of things Clint seems to know about," she added mysteriously. Before anyone could ask what she meant, she was quick to change the subject. "By the way, Mom, can I borrow the camera this afternoon. I uh… wanted to get some shots of the rodeo."

"Sure," her mother nodded. "Just take it with you at rodeo time."

"Well, actually, Mom," Jenny said, almost too casually, "I kind of need it now… I want to get some pictures of the puppy," she added quickly.

"No problem, just don't lose it," her mother replied with a sideways glance at her husband. Both of them knew that something wasn't being said and both knew equally well that no amount of cajoling would pry whatever it was out of their headstrong daughter. In any event, there wasn't time to think about it. There was just time for a bite of lunch before they had to start getting ready for the rodeo performance. "Why don't you three shoo outside with that pup until we can get some lunch on," Laura Douglas directed.

Jenny, camera in hand, Josh and Clayton with Casey underarm bounced out of the camper.

As Roy moved his papers from the table and began to set dishes in place for the upcoming meal, he glanced out the window. There, huddled in a little circle on the grass with the puppy in the middle, Josh, Jenny and Clayton had been joined by Clint Runner who seemed to appear and disappear like a phantom. The four of them were engaged in what was evidently a very confidential conversation.

"I wonder what those kids are up to," Roy puzzled aloud. "There's something going on, that's for sure.

"Oh probably just some prank they're planning," his wife responded lightly. "You know what kids are like."

"Maybe," Roy said, turning away from the window, but he wasn't convinced.

Later, Laura extended an invitation to Clint to join them for lunch, but the boy declined shyly and was suddenly gone. Lunch was a quiet affair as everyone seemed deep in thought. Communication was at a minimum.

The meal was quickly dispensed with and it was time to get the stock ready for the rodeo. Roy, Josh and Clayton hurried away to get started. Jenny begged off in order to look after the pup and her dad agreed, saying he would have enough help from the boys and Ben.

It wasn't long until the rodeo was underway. At that point, Clayton, who was riding that afternoon, became the focus of attention. The scores had been excellent in the Boys' Steer Riding and it looked like he would have to score in the high 70s to be among the top four steer riders who would go to the pay window. Watching the first couple of steer riders as he resined his bull-rope, Clayton was more nervous than usual.

Josh noticed his cousin's anxiety and came over to offer encouragement.

"I think you've got a good one here, C. J. Ride him like you can and you'll get some of that prize money," he told him.

Clayton smiled at hearing the nickname. It was rapidly catching on around the rodeo circuit.

"Some of the prize money? I'm goin' for top spot, Cousin, so look out," he replied.

"That's the right attitude," Josh responded, with

a friendly punch on the shoulder. "Hey, you won't be winning anything without a cowbell on that rope."

"Geez," Clayton groaned, "I left it in the camper. I'll go get it. Will you drop my rope on my steer when they run him in?"

"You bet," replied Josh, "but you better hurry."

Clayton was off in a flash out the back door of the arena and heading for the area behind the arena where the trucks, campers and horse trailers were parked. He was cutting between two pick-ups when he saw a horse being backed out of a trailer.

Stopping, Clayton noticed that the trailer belonged to Jud Parradine, the former World Champion Cowboy who had won the Calgary Stampede earlier that summer. The trailer was not easy to miss with the words "Jud Parradine, World Champion Calf Roper" emblazoned on the sides. Clayton had met Jud, who like many of the cowboys, was friends with Uncle Roy and decided he would stop and say a fast hello. At first, Clayton couldn't see the cowboy as he was hidden by the horse.

He heard a familiar voice speaking softly to calm the horse, "Okay, Boy, come on now, this will just take a minute. We're just going to find a new home for you for a little while. We can't be lettin' our ol' buddy Jud win another rodeo, now can we?"

The man, still hidden from Clayton's view, began leading the horse away from the trailer and through the maze of vehicles parked around it. Clayton realized that he was witnessing first-hand the latest in the series of "marauder" incidents; that whoever was leading the horse away from Jud Parradine's trailer was kidnapping the horse to prevent Jud from winning.

As the mysterious cowboy came around the long, red four-horse trailer, he and Clayton suddenly came face to face.

The marauder was Len Tucker!

Chapter Nineteen

For a long moment the cowboy and the young boy looked at each other. Finally, Len Tucker broke the silence. "I'm sorry you had to be the one to find out, Clayton," he said, his voice displaying no anger, only a kind of sadness.

"Y...Y...You," the boy was finally able to stammer, "Of all people, I never thought it could be..."

"I know, kid," Len interrupted, holding up a hand. "I have trouble believing it myself sometimes, but that's the way it is. The question is, what do we do now?"

"But why?" Clayton asked, his eyes welling up with tears as he realized one of his heroes wasn't a hero at all. "Why would you do all those things? You're one of the best cowboys in the world, you don't have to!"

"*One* of the best, Clayton, that's just the thing," Len tried to explain, "One of the best, but never the best. I guess I just couldn't stand being second man on the totem pole anymore. I wanted to be number one, just once. Maybe someday you'll understand."

"I don't think so. I don't think I'll ever understand," Clayton shook his head angrily. "I'd rather be second my whole life than have to cheat to be first."

Clayton turned and ran through the trailers and trucks to the Douglas camper. He retrieved the missing cowbell and was off again back to the arena, careful to take a different route so as not to meet up with Len again.

As he ran up to the chutes, he heard Hank Parker calling his name over the P.A. system. "Clayton Findlay, last call, your stock is in the chutes."

Clayton saw Josh standing on the back of the chute beckoning furiously for him to hurry. Clayton rushed up and threw the cowbell to Josh who quickly fastened it to the bull-rope, while Clayton tightened his chaps.

"What kept ya?" Josh asked him.

"Tell ya later," Clayton replied, climbing up and into the chute.

"Okay, now you're the last guy, and a 76 will get you into the money. Let's see you do it," Josh clapped his cousin on the back.

Clayton climbed down on the steer and Josh helped him with his rope. He was just about ready to nod his head to have the gate opened when the figure of Len Tucker dropped into the chute alongside him.

Len leaned forward and said softly, "Just one favor, Clayton, please don't tell anyone until after the rodeo...please."

No one else heard Len's words and as Clayton looked up he saw sorrow and pain in the face of the cowboy he had once admired.

"Okay," he agreed grimly. The boy then slid up on his rope, gritted his teeth and nodded quickly.

Eight seconds of blurring, bone-jarring, teeth-rattling, arm-wrenching action ended as they had started, with the young cowboy firmly in place on the back of the steer that had tried everything to put its unwelcome rider on the ground. After the klaxon, Clayton dismounted right at the feet of Tub Willoughby who signalled safe, baseball style, and then helped the steer rider to his feet.

Clayton retrieved his rope and was walking back to the chutes when he heard the voice of Hank Parker boom out over the microphone.

"Seventy-seven points for young Clayton Findlay and that means that this cowboy will wind up in fourth place, with Josh Douglas the winner of the event."

Josh was first to reach Clayton and pumped his cousin's hand up and down in hearty congratulations.

The kid from Toronto had placed for the first time at a rodeo and despite the unpleasantness with Len Tucker a few minutes earlier, Clayton beamed with pride and pleasure. Uncle Roy also came up and shook hands and offered congratulations to both boys.

"Looks like I've got a couple of pretty good hands to keep my eye on in the future," he noted with pride, then turned to get the next event underway.

During the Ladies Barrel Racing which followed, Clayton craned his neck in every direction to try and catch sight of Len Tucker. He wondered what Len had in mind in asking him to hold off telling anyone what he had seen. Did the cowboy intend to carry on as if nothing had happened? Clayton doubted that. What then? Had he simply packed up and run off? Or did he plan to deny everything and say Clayton was mistaken?

One thing was for sure. Clayton wouldn't have to wait long for the answers to his questions. Calf Roping was the next event and Len Tucker was scheduled to rope last.

As the Barrel Racing concluded and the arena was being cleared, Josh jumped up on the fence alongside his cousin.

"You're looking mighty thoughtful," he said.

"Yeah, I guess I was just thinking about Len Tucker," Clayton replied.

"That's funny, so was I," countered Josh.

"Really?" Clayton wondered if somehow Josh was aware of what Len had been up to.

"Yeah, I was just thinking, if he could just place this afternoon, he'll qualify for the Canadian Finals in two events and that would give him a heck of a chance at the All-Round this year. Maybe his best chance ever."

So that was it, Clayton thought to himself. If Len were to win the roping here at Morley and go on to the Finals, maybe he could still win the All-Round Championship, even if he was found out.

The first roper was ready and Clayton leaned forward in anticipation of what was about to happen, though he wasn't at all sure what that would be.

The third man out was Jud Parradine and sure enough, he was aboard his own horse as if nothing at all had happened. Jud had a good run and took the lead with a time of ten seconds flat.

The second last man to go would be Lefty Shivers who, true to his name, roped and tied with his left hand. Shivers was fast today, even faster than Jud Parradine and turned in a 9.9. Shivers had the lead with only Len Tucker left to rope.

Finally, Clayton caught sight of the familiar figure of his former friend, mounted and moving into position behind the barrier.

The crowd, the other cowboys, everyone tensed as the big cowboy sat motionless, his eyes glued to the calf he was to rope. He nodded his head and the calf was released. Len Tucker gave chase. His rope snaked out, found its target and the cowboy was off his horse and down the rope.

In spite of everything that had happened, Clayton couldn't help but feel the excitement mounting in himself as he realized he was watching the fastest exhibition of calf roping he had ever seen—maybe that anyone had ever seen.

In one fluid motion, Len Tucker threw the calf to the ground, dropped the loop end of the piggin string over one of the calf's legs and brought up the two hind legs.

"He's gonna be under eight seconds," Josh breathed in disbelief.

A buzz in the crowd was beginning to crescendo as everyone realized they were witnessing what had the makings of a spectacular time. Len's hands moved gracefully in the motion they had performed so many times before. One wrap, two wraps and a half-hitch. And then it happened. Just as he was about to put the final knot on his tie with plenty of time to spare to win, he stopped!

His right hand in mid-air, left hand on the calf, Len Tucker stopped.

"Come on, finish it!" Josh urged.

The cowboy paused, looked up and then almost as quickly as he had thrown the calf and tied it, he untied it and let it go. A groan went up from the crowd as the animal scurried off. The calf, at least, was happy with the turn of events. Len Tucker stood up and led his horse slowly to the chutes where Josh and Clayton were now standing.

The voice of Hank Parker was subdued as he spoke to the crowd. "I don't know what happened there folks, it looked like a great run, maybe a record-setting run, but it will be a `no time' for that cowboy."

Len got to the chutes just as Roy rode up and dismounted.

"What happened, Len?" Roy asked him.

164

"I just retired from rodeo, Roy," Tucker told him simply.

"Retired, are you kidding? This is the best shot you ever had at the All-Round. It's practically in the bag," Roy told him incredulously.

"I know that but I don't deserve it," Len said, his head down, his voice almost inaudible.

"What do you mean?" Roy inquired.

"Well… you see…" Len looked over at Clayton, then back at Roy, "You see I'm the guy that's been stealing horses and sabotaging cowboys' runs. I did all those things so I could win the All-Round.

"I just couldn't stand the idea of finishing second one more time," the cowboy shook his head sadly, "but I guess I realize now that it wouldn't be much of a championship if I won it that way. The horses I stole are out at my place. I've been looking after them; they're in as good shape as when I took `em. I was planning to get them back to their owners after the season was over."

"You know we'll have to inform the law about this, Len," Roy told his long-time friend.

"I know, Roy. Do what you have to do," Len replied, "but I've got one favor to ask," he added.

"What's that?" Roy asked.

"I want to try Bad Medicine," Len said quietly. "I know it'll be the last ride I'll ever make and I probably can't ride him. But he's the greatest bull that's ever bucked in this country and I've never been on him. I'd feel mighty proud to end my career that way. And there's one more thing I want you to know, I never had anything to do with any of the stuff that's been happening at the D Lazy D. I give you my word."

Roy hesitated and looked at Len Tucker a long time before he replied.

165

"You promise to stick around when the rodeo's over?" he demanded.

"I won't run, Roy," was the reply.

"Well, in that case," Roy looked at Clayton and Josh who both nodded their approval. "In that case, you better get your bull-rope 'cause you've got a bull to ride."

Only four people in Morley that day knew that Len Tucker was making his last ride. As the cowboy was placing his rope around the bull's huge girth, Roy was there helping him get ready. Josh and Clayton were perched on the back of the chute offering encouragement.

As soon as he was ready, Len paused, took a deep breath and nodded his head The gate was flung open. As he had with Lefty Shivers, Bad Medicine started with an incredibly high first jump, landing like a massive sledge hammer at the end of it. Normally that first jump put cowboys in trouble but Len Tucker had weathered the storm, at least so far.

The second jump followed and in mid-air the bull began its spin. As it hit the ground a blurring spin to the left followed. Still Len was aboard, though not quite as firmly as he had been. The centrifugal force of the bull's lightning fast spin was forcing the rider over to the right.

Then, with incredible dexterity, the bull leaped out of the spin into another high jump, again crashing down hard on its front feet. Now Len Tucker was in serious trouble, having been flung down on the bull's right shoulder.

As Bad Medicine whipped back to the right, his head struck the cowboy hard in the face. Still Len Tucker refused to give up and with a superhuman effort hauled himself back up onto the middle of the bull's back.

The klaxon sounded just as the bull finally succeeded in breaking the cowboy's grip on his rope and threw him hard to the ground. But he had made it. Len Tucker, making his last ride, had ridden the bull nobody had ever ridden.

And now he stood in the middle of the arena, his face bloodied, and acknowledged the cheers of the crowd as Hank Parker announced above the roar that the score for the ride was a remarkable 93 points. No one cheered any louder than Roy and Josh and Clayton.

It had taken a long time but Len Tucker had done something no man had ever done. Although he would not win the All-Round Championship, people would no longer remember him as the man who always came second.

He was a champion that day.

Chapter Twenty

Len Tucker was as good as his word. The rodeo was barely over and the championship buckles presented when the cowboy, an intensely serious look on the usually cheerful face, presented himself to Roy. He was accompanied by about ten other cowboys.

Roy recognized them as most of the men who had been victimized over the season by the marauder incidents. Len Tucker must have acted quickly to get them together before they headed for home. Only Lefty Shivers was conspicuous by his absence.

"Mind if I handle this, Roy?" Len asked.

"No, Len, I don't mind," Roy answered his long-time friend. "You handle it however you want."

Len nodded and quickly climbed up on the fence where he could easily be seen and heard.

"Boys, I don't aim to keep you long," he addressed the gathering. "What I'm about to tell you, Roy here already knows. Every one of you fellas, at some time or other this season has had a rope go missing or tampered with or some other piece of equipment sabotaged. Some of you have even lost horses. It's about time you find out who's responsible for all of those incidents." Len paused and looked at Roy.

Then taking a deep breath and letting it out slowly, he said in a voice barely above a whisper, "I am."

Instantly a threatening murmur ran through the knot of cowboys.

Roy spoke up. "Hold on a second, men. I know you're all plenty upset and you have every right to be. But all your horses are safe and have been looked after. Now, I'm not defending Len," Roy went on, "but I think we need to look at this with clear heads. He's made a bad mistake, but as far as I'm concerned he's taken one step toward making up for that mistake right here."

"Look," Len went on, "I know I messed up. I had some kind of idea that the All-Round Championship was more important than a man's honor."

Tears came to the cowboy's eyes as he added, "Or his friends. Today I realized how wrong I was." Len glanced at Clayton who along with Josh and Jenny were standing to one side of the group.

Turning back to the cluster of cowboys, he said, "I haven't spent one dime of the prize money I won when I cheated." Len Tucker's voice cracked with emotion. "I'll be giving that money to Roy to split up between you."

With that, Len climbed down from the fence and crossed to Roy. "You'd best be calling the R.C.M.P., Roy. I'm ready."

Roy looked at Len, dragged a shirt sleeve across his chin and turned to the gathered cowboys. "Fellas, I don't know a whole lot about the law," he spoke slowly, carefully measuring his words. "It seems to me it's up to you. You'll be getting back your horses and equipment and your share of the prize money. Len's already told me he'll never compete again. Now what you have to decide is whether that's enough or whether you want this man to go to jail," Roy told them pointedly. "The decision is yours."

Throughout the group, men kicked at the arena dirt with well-worn boots. Some looked at each other. Others looked at the man they had all come

169

to like. World Champion Jud Parradine was the first to speak. "I have no reason to persecute a man. As far as I'm concerned, the matter's over and done with," he drawled.

Jame Gartens, another all-round contender, added, "Yep, that's the way I feel, too."

Phil Streeter, whose horse at been stolen at Taber, spoke next. "I'm satisfied to get my horse back. I ain't a man to look for revenge just for its own sake."

And so it went. Every member of the group agreed not to pursue the matter further and, gradually, quietly, the meeting broke up. Len had promised to personally return horses and property to their rightful owners within a week.

When they had all gone, Len turned to Roy. "I want to thank you," he said simply. "I know you didn't have to do that."

"I'm afraid you're not out of the woods yet," Roy warned him. "There's still one fly in the ointment and that fly's named Lefty Shivers. If he wants to press charges, there's nothing we can do. I'm afraid it'll go badly for you."

Len Tucker winced. "I'd forgotten about him. We've never had much use for each other. I don't think I've got much of a chance with Shivers."

"I think you're probably right," Roy agreed ruefully. "It might be better if I talk to him."

Suddenly Jenny, who had to this point been standing quietly with Josh and Clayton, spoke up. "Lefty Shivers might not be as big a problem as you think, Dad," she grinned at the two surprised men.

"Jenny's right. I think Lefty might be persuaded to see reason," Josh added.

"Especially if we talk to him," Clayton put in.

"Wait a minute," Roy interrupted. "What are you three talking about? Lefty Shivers is nobody to fool with."

"We know that Dad," Josh said seriously. "We won't do anything foolish. I promise. Just give us fifteen minutes with our friend Mr. Shivers, and a lot of troubles will be over."

Roy paused a long time and studied each of the youngsters carefully before replying. "All right," he consented reluctantly. "I know you're all responsible kids. I'll give you fifteen minutes... no more."

"Thanks, Dad," Jenny called over her shoulder as the three youngsters turned and sped off toward the camper parking lot. A couple of minutes later, they slowed to a walk as they came in sight of the Shivers camper, conspicuous for the three months of black dirt accumulated on its sides. Slowly, Josh, Jenny and Clayton came around the camper. Lefty Shivers was throwing his bronc riding saddle in the back of his pickup. Miles was lounging on the ground next to the camper. It looked like they were almost ready to leave.

"Hi fellas!" Josh sang out cheerfully.

"Sure glad we caught you before you left," Clayton grinned. "We would have hated for you to go without our getting a chance to say goodbye."

Miles climbed to his feet. "Take a hike why don't ya?" he growled.

"I've got no time to waste on you punks," Lefty snorted, gathering the last of his equipment. "So beat it."

"Why don't you..." Jenny's words were cut short by a well-placed elbow to the ribs from Josh.

"Actually," he interrupted her with syrupy pleasantness in his voice, "it wouldn't really be a waste of time talking to us. We just dropped by to tell you the news. Course, if you're too busy…" Josh turned on his heel and began to leave. Jenny and Clayton fell in behind him.

"Hey, wait a minute." Lefty called. "What news are you talking about?"

Josh, Jenny and Clayton turned again to face the two brothers.

"Oh you mean you haven't heard?" Josh slowly walked over to where Lefty was leaning against the truck. "It seems Len Tucker just confessed to all the rodeo crimes, the missing ropes, broken equipment, stolen horses - the works."

"Tucker!" Lefty whistled in surprise. His face broke into an unpleasant grin. "Well, I'll be," he chortled. "How about that, little brother, good ol' Len Tucker a common criminal. Now ain't that a shame."

Miles Shivers laughed gleefully at his brother's sarcastic words. "Aw, that's too bad," he added in the same tone of voice.

Jenny rose to Len's defense. "Well, he said he'd get the horses back to their owners and give back the prize money and…"

"Well, that's real nice of him," Lefty sneered, "but that ain't gonna get that little ol' worm off the hook, no way."

"Actually, Lefty," Clayton pointed out, "Everybody's agreed to just let it drop. No one is going to the law."

"Is that so?" Lefty Shivers laughed. "Well, I'm afraid a law-abiding citizen like me just has no choice but to turn that snake in."

"Yeah, they'll probably put him away for quite some time," Miles' nasal voice intoned.

172

"Well, Lefty, we were hoping you'd see it differently," Josh said quietly. "Everybody makes mistakes."

"Yeah," Jenny spoke up suddenly. "Some people even cut off horse's tails."

Miles gulped and his face turned the color of an overripe apple. Lefty straightened up. "What are you talking about?" he sputtered.

"Speaking of mistakes," Josh interrupted. "It seems you made one here today."

Lefty turned defiant. "Is that so? And what would that be, punk?" he spat out.

From out of her pocket, Jenny produced a snapshot — one she had taken that very day with her mother's Polaroid camera. She held it up for Lefty and Miles to see. In the picture, Lefty was stretched over a corral fence, poised to insert a hypodermic needle into the side of a bull wearing the D Lazy D brand.

"Gimme that," Lefty snatched the picture from her hand.

"No need to grab, Lefty," Jenny said sweetly. "I was going to present you with it as a gift. I have three more just as good in our camper."

As the foul-tempered cowboy fumed, Miles said, "Don't believe her Lefty, she's lying."

"Don't bet on it, Miles," Josh said coldly. "Now I think it's time we talked about a deal.

"You figure it's your legal duty to report Len to the police. I'm sure you'll understand that we have to look at this little matter of you trying to sabotage the D Lazy D the same way." Josh paused to let Lefty Shivers digest his words.

"Of course," Josh went on, "we might be willing to forget all about this if you could see your way clear to forget about pressing charges against Len."

Clayton and Jenny were having trouble hiding their amazement at seeing a coldly determined side of Josh they had never known existed.

Lefty Shivers' face had drained of all of its color. His fury was such that it looked as if at any minute, his evil eyes would pop out of his head. His whole body trembled with rage.

"I'll want all of the pictures," he finally sputtered, trying to regain his control.

"Uh-uh," Josh shook his head. "No way. We'll hang on to those and if one more thing should ever happen at the D Lazy D, then those pictures will be delivered to the R.C.M.P. in a hurry."

"Do you understand, Lefty?" Clayton asked pointedly, picking up on Josh's cue.

The cowboy's shoulders slumped in defeat. "Yeah, I understand."

"Lefty," Miles whined. "You're not going to let them get away with…"

"Shut up!" his brother snapped.

"That includes anything happening to any of our animals," Jenny added pointedly.

"What are you talking about?" Miles sneered.

"She's talking about how we'd be forced to drop in on the R.C.M.P. with some interesting photos if any of our animals got sick," Clayton explained threateningly.

"Or shot," Josh added, cold fury in his voice.

"Are you accusing us of…?" Miles took a step forward.

"Shut yer mouth, I told ya," Lefty snapped at his younger brother. "You got a deal, Douglas. No pictures, no problems."

174

"I though you might see it that way," Josh smiled grimly at his two adversaries. "Much as we'd like to stick around and visit longer, we've got to be going. We knew you'd want to be brought up to date on all the news."

"Oh, and you can keep the picture, Lefty," Jenny chirped. "I think I caught your best side, don't you?"

"So long, fellas, see ya down the road," Clayton called as he and his two cousins turned away.

They made it back to their own camper with two minutes to spare before Roy's deadline. The laughter of Roy and Len was loud and long as the threesome recounted the story of their encounter with the Shivers boys.

"I'm mighty proud of you kids," Roy told them. "I knew there was something you weren't telling me this morning. Come to think of it, I should have known something was up when I didn't see Jenny around the rodeo all day, not even when Clayton was riding."

"I was hiding in some bales beside the bulls all afternoon," Jenny explained. "I didn't want to miss my chance."

"But how did you know they were going to pull something today?" Len queried.

"Clint Runner tipped me off this morning when I went to his house to get the puppy," Jenny answered him.

"So you were cooking all this up this morning when I saw you outside the camper," Roy recalled.

"Right," Clayton beamed. "The pictures were my idea."

"I always kind of thought Clint was in with those Shivers varmints," Len mused.

"I guess he could have gone either way," Josh explained. "But when he heard Miles bragging about shooting Casey, he made up his mind. When he heard them planning to drug some of the bulls, he decided to let us know."

"Funny thing is," Roy seemed puzzled. "The bulls bucked just fine today."

"Somebody came along and Lefty was scared off," Jenny said. "I don't even think he actually got the needle into that first bull."

"You must have worked fast to get four pictures," Clayton told her admiringly.

"I'll say one thing," Roy Douglas grinned. "You sure did a good job of not letting on about anything."

"Well, it's a girl's right to have a few secrets," Jenny said.

As the laughter swelled again, she thought to herself that one secret she would never be able to tell anyone was that there weren't any other pictures of Lefty Shivers. There just hadn't been time to get any more. It's a good thing her bluff had worked. Looking down at Casey nestled contentedly in her lap, she joined in the laughter.

Chapter Twenty-One

Clayton Findlay's stay in the west and the Canadian rodeo season came to a simultaneous and fitting end at the Canadian Finals Rodeo in Edmonton. For weeks, Clayton had looked forward to the CFR which was staged every November in the magnificent Edmonton Coliseum. The top ten cowboys in each event over the course of the season would be meeting in sudden-death competition over six performances to determine the Canadian Champions.

In the Boys' Steer Riding event, only the top six riders for the season went to the Finals. Josh was among them, having finished up in fourth place for the season.

Clayton wasn't disappointed by his first encounter with the CFR. The color and pageantry of the Northlands Coliseum, home of the Finals, the thousands of cheering spectators, and the tension that pulsed through the entire arena all combined to make the Canadian Finals one of the most exciting events in his young life.

The boy was especially thrilled by the performances of the bucking stock that had been brought to the Finals. Some of the greatest horses and bulls in all of North America were there. As had been the case at the Calgary Stampede, only the best animals of each stock contractor were selected. For the Finals, the cowboys themselves voted for the stock they would compete on.

The Douglas outfit was well represented with fourteen bucking horses, including three of Doc Holliday's colts and ten bulls, with Bad Medicine at the top of the list, all having been selected for Canadian Rodeo's most important week.

After three CFR performances, it was evident that Josh was not going to win the Steer Riding Championship. In all of the events, contestants received 40 points for a win, then 30, 20 and 10 for the remaining spots in the top four each night. So far, Josh had collected just 30 points for a third and a fourth, while one contestant, Kelly Vanderlea of Rocky Mountain House, had accumulated 110 points with two firsts and a second in the three go-rounds.

Nevertheless, Josh was anything but disappointed by the results thus far. "It's my first Finals and I'm plenty glad to get this far," he told Clayton. "This is Kelly's last time here—he'll be too old next year—and the way he's riding, he deserves to be the champion."

Clayton, Jenny and Josh arrived at the Coliseum early on Saturday afternoon for the fourth performance. The boys liked to make use of every opportunity to rub shoulders with the competitors, stock contractors, clowns and rodeo officials. They were talking with a group of bareback riders when Roy strode up with a broad grin on his face.

"Clayton, I've got a mighty big surprise for you," he beamed.

"What is it, Uncle Roy?" the boy inquired, looking at Josh who merely shrugged to indicate he didn't know what was up.

"Look," Uncle Roy said and pointed behind him to a tall, slender man in a blue shirt and grey stetson walking towards them.

"Dad!" Clayton shouted, completely taken by surprise at the unexpected arrival. Mr. Findlay moved forward and grasped his son by the shoulders. The two met in the awkward embrace of a father and a boy growing up. For a moment neither the boy nor his father spoke for fear their voices might betray their emotions. Finally, it was Clayton who broke the silence.

"You look great, Dad. I don't think I've ever seen you in anything but a three-piece suit," he said quietly.

"Three-piece suits don't make it at rodeos, son," Mr. Findlay smiled. "Especially when you're surrounded by cowboys."

Clayton nodded and smiled as he thought back to his first encounter with the west and his disdain at that time for western clothes and manners. Now he was completely at home in western shirts and a battered straw cowboy hat. Clayton realized his life would never again be the same.

"You couldn't have timed it any better, Dad," Clayton said as his father and Josh shook hands. "You'll be able to sit with me for the rodeo. Aunt Laura's going shopping to-day, so her seat will be empty. We'll be right behind the chutes so we can get a real good look at Josh in the Steer Riding."

"Well, maybe we better get up to those seats. The rodeo should be starting right away," Mr. Findlay said, his hand on his son's shoulder.

"Good luck, Josh," Clayton said earnestly to his cousin.

"Go get `em," echoed Mr. Findlay.

Josh acknowledged their encouragement with a wave as Clayton and his dad headed for their seats. Jenny meandered in behind the chutes to visit with the girls who had made the Finals in Barrel Racing. Although Jenny wasn't a finalist, she knew her time would come.

For the next two and one-half hours Clayton regaled his father with the news of the summer, interspersed with explanations of what was taking place in the arena. Clayton recalled for his Dad the incident with the bull in the corral at the D Lazy D.

He went on to describe his first rodeo, the prairie fire and Hector Levy, the Calgary Stampede, his first steer ride and the mysterious series of events that had plagued the rodeo circuit until Len Tucker had been exposed as the culprit. He told his father that for the following season, Len would be joining Ben Bradley as a pickup man for his uncle Roy's outfit. He and his father laughed at how the Shivers boys had been bested. But most of all, the boy from the east talked about a black maverick horse called Doc Holliday.

Mr. Findlay listened patiently, acknowledging that it must have indeed been a very exciting summer. Then it was time for the Boys' Steer Riding. Clayton and his father both strained forward in their seats to get a good look at the action. Josh was first out and marked 75 points on a good steer. It looked like the score might hold up for first place for the day until Kelly Vanderlea on the final steer received a 77 for his third win.

Still, Josh had collected 30 points. Although Kelly Vanderlea had clinched the championship with his ride, Josh was now just 10 points out of second place, held by his old adversary, Miles Shivers.

In the Bull Riding, Bad Medicine unceremoniously tossed Lefty Shivers to the ground in a rematch of their Taber meeting. It was a great way to end the rodeo and Clayton felt exhilarated as he and his father relaxed in their seats and waited for Roy, Jenny and Josh to join them.

"Son, I've come to take you back home," Mr. Findlay said simply as they watched the crowd leaving the Coliseum.

Clayton looked at his father for a long time. The resentment he had once felt at having been sent west had long since disappeared. Suddenly, the last six months of his life seemed like a dream, a dream that was about to come to an end. He thought about Toronto, his friends and his mother. He realized that he missed his home but that the west had become a very important part of his life, a part of his life that he must now give up. The thought gave him mixed feelings.

"It's funny, isn't it," he said slowly, "when I first got here I would have given anything for you to come and get me. Now I love it here. As much as I miss you and Mom and home, it's really going to be hard for me to leave." Tears welled up in Clayton's eyes.

"I understand how you feel son, but I'm sure you'll be able to adjust back to Toronto life," Mr. Findlay responded gently.

"I don't want you to think I don't want to be with you, it's just … it's just…" Clayton fumbled for words.

"No need to explain son, I really do understand," Mr. Findlay said reassuringly.

They sat in silence for awhile and then were joined by Roy, Josh and Jenny. The five of them went out for supper between performances, but Clayton did little more than pick at his food.

Saturday night's rodeo and the final performance Sunday afternoon came and went. Except for when Josh passed Miles Shivers and finished up in second place for the finals, Clayton was unable to muster much enthusiasm.

The ride back to the ranch was a mixture of exhilaration and sadness. Clayton was as quiet as he had been those first days after his arrival at the D Lazy D.

Sunday night he and his Dad packed their things in order to catch the eastbound train early the next morning. Roy had suggested the train trip to allow the two time to get re-acquainted and Mr. Findlay had liked the idea.

Clayton spent his final evening at the D Lazy D walking slowly around the now familiar ranch. He wanted the time alone. It was difficult coming to grips with having to leave behind a way of life that had become so important to him.

His last stop was at the corral of Doc Holliday. He slipped up on the horse's back and lay forward on the massive neck. "Well, Doc, I guess we had some pretty good times, huh?" The boy's voice was husky with emotion. "I won't ever forget you Doc," Clayton whispered. "I hope you won't ever forget me."

The stallion nickered softly as if to reply. Overhead, the clear western night sky was a spectacular mass of tiny sparkling dots. Clayton looked up, picked out the brightest star and fervently made a wish. Then, with a hint of an early chinook wind at his back, Clayton Findlay made his way slowly back to the house.

The next morning Clayton found himself back at the train station where it had all begun several months before. The station was crowded as he and his dad, Uncle Roy, Aunt Laura and Josh and Jenny worked their way toward the platform. Cindy McKannin had come too; the normally bubbly barrel racer was unusually subdued as the time for departure approached. Clayton wished that just once he could have spent a few minutes alone with her. Here he was going away and he still didn't really know if she even liked him or not. He thought she did, but with girls, you could never really be sure.

At the steps of the train, Clayton stopped, turned and took a deep breath. He was determined that this would be a brave good-bye. "I'll miss your apple pie," he said, giving his aunt an affectionate hug. "And I'll really miss you."

"Take good care of yourself, Clayton," Aunt Laura replied, with her familiar smile.

"Uncle Roy, I don't know how to thank you for all you've done for me," Clayton said to the man who had been like a father to him.

"No thanks necessary, Clayton. We were glad to have you," Roy responded.

"Good-bye Cindy," Clayton said hurriedly, wishing he had the courage to show her how he felt.

Cindy didn't reply but grasped Clayton by the shoulders and kissed him quickly but firmly on the mouth. Then she said, "I'll miss you, Clayton."

"You are...I mean you will?" Clayton sputtered. "That's... that's great... I mean... well, I'm going to miss you too." And he kissed her back.

As usual, it was Jenny who brought the romantic moment to an end. "What about me?" she griped. "I wouldn't mind a kiss myself, ya know." Clayton laughed and leaned forward to kiss the freckled cheek. "Take good care of Doc Holliday for me," he said. "And Casey too... even if she is a girl."

As Clayton turned to Josh, he could feel the tears burning their way into his eyes. Josh, too, was having a difficult time controlling his emotion.

"So long, Josh," Clayton thrust out his hand.

"So long," his cousin replied in a barely audible voice.

"Oh. I almost forgot," Mr. Findlay interrupted. "There's something I should tell you before we get on the train. Your Uncle Roy told me he'll be needing a good hand around the D Lazy D next summer and he was wondering if I'd let you come out here. I told him I thought it would be okay. I hope you don't mind."

Mr. Findlay barely had the words out of his mouth when Josh, Clayton, Jenny and Cindy were whooping with joy. Anyone seeing the four of them bounding and jumping around the platform would have thought they had all just won their events at the Calgary Stampede.

Suddenly Clayton stopped and became very serious. "I don't know if it's such a good idea, Josh."

"Are you kidding, why not?" exclaimed his cousin.

"Well, if I come out here for the whole summer, you aren't gonna win nearly as many rodeos," Clayton dead-panned, with a playful wink at a beaming Cindy.

"I guess I'll just have to take that chance, C. J.," Josh grinned.

And with a last wave, the two travellers disappeared into the train, with Clayton Findlay explaining to his Dad the feeling a cowboy gets as he is about to make his ride and hears the announcer say, "Out of chute number two, the next cowboy is C.J. Findlay."

You can use the coupon below to order any book in the trilogy or ALL THREE AT THE SPECIAL MONEY-SAVING PRICE.

Please send ___ autographed copies of
The Cowboy Kid @ $7.50 each
      (includes G.S.T) $_____

Please send ___ autographed copies of
Ride for the Crown @ $7.50 each
      (includes G.S.T.) $_____

Please send ___ autographed copies of
Ride the High Country @ $7.50 each
      (includes G.S.T.) $_____

***If ordering all three books, send
just $21.40 per set. (Includes G.S.T.)

                      $_____

Shipping and Handling $ 3.00

TOTAL $_____

Send book order coupon to:

Red Hawk Books
Box 5053
High River, Alberta
T1V 1M3

See next page for information on other titles in series
185

Collect all three books in the Rodeo Trilogy

Brand new editions of David A. Poulsen's bestselling first book The Cowboy Kid and the popular sequel Ride for the Crown are now available from Red Hawk Books. And, at last, the long-awaited third book in the RODEO TRILOGY, Ride the High Country is also available to fans of the first two.

The Cowboy Kid

Somebody is out to sabotage the rodeo. The show-down is looming and Clayton Findlay is right in the middle.

Forced to leave his beloved Toronto to spend the summer on his uncle's ranch in southern Alberta, the reluctant easterner is suddenly thrust into the world of cowboys, bucking broncs, wild bulls...and mystery!

Gradually the big city kid begins to appreciate and even love his surroundings and after finding an un-likely friend in an untamed rodeo stallion, Clayton earns the respect and friendship of the cowboys and cowgirls who now make up his world.

He gets a new name, "C.J.", takes up riding steers in the rodeo and teams up with his cousins Josh and Jenny to tackle the mystery of the rodeo marauder. And along the way Clayton Findlay becomes The Cowboy Kid.

Ride for the Crown

C.J. Findlay once again teams up with cousins Josh and Jenny to ride the rodeo circuit and to try to solve the latest mystery to hit the D Lazy D.

When a strange boy suddenly arrives at the ranch wearing odd clothes and carrying a satchel full of money, no one is quite sure how to react.

Soon C.J., Josh and Jenny find themselves in the middle of an international incident involving the evil, power-seeking Baron Steg and a ruthless group of followers who will stop at nothing to get their hands on the mysterious newcomer. The action takes C.J. and his western family from the coast of British Columbia to the skyscrapers of Toronto as they try to reunite a European Prince with his father.

The result is the latest exciting adventure from popular Alberta writer David A. Poulsen. You won't want to put this one down!

Ride the High Country

What seems like an innocent vacation to the tiny Principality of Mendenstein tucked high in the Bavarian Alps turns out to be most dangerous mystery yet for the Cowboy Kid, C.J. Findlay, and the rest of the gang from the D Lazy D.

Baron Steg, the villainous adversary C.J. and cousins Josh and Jenny met up with in *Ride for the Crown*, is back, with an even nastier and deadlier means to achieve his goal—the overthrow of the peaceful country .

Can a mystical falcon and an unfriendly mountain man help C.J. and the others thwart the evil Baron? A breathtaking chase through the mountain passes of Mendenstein is the last hope. *Ride the High Country* is filled with fast-paced, suspenseful action that will keep you turning pages long into the night.

About the Author

A former rodeo competitor and rodeo clown, David A. Poulsen is a freelance writer and broadcaster. His short story The Welcomin' won the Alberta Culture Story Writing Competition in 1984. Since then he has written plays, a collection of short stories, *Dream*, a novel, *Don't Fence Me In*, and the sports biography, *Robokicker*, co-written with Saskatchewan Roughrider placekicker, Dave Ridgway. This is the second edition of his popular Young Adult Rodeo Trilogy which includes David's bestselling first book, *The Cowboy Kid*, *Ride for the Crown* and *Ride the High Country*. David lives near High River, Alberta where he raises quarter horses and is at work on two novels.